I stood up and b ..

This is no concern of

"What makes you

teeth to make a shar

thought he was smil

snickering up his sleeve and, whatever it was, the joke was on me.

"No client, no money, no case." I tossed back at him. "I don't do charity work."

"I think this is yours." He held an evidence bag with an envelope in it between his forefinger and thumb. My name was scrawled in purple curlicue letters across the envelope. The only other mark was the Bayside Hotel logo. A piece of note paper was in another evidence bag.

"What are those?"

"An envelope and letter."

"Where did you find them?" That envelope had all the charm of a spitting python. I could sense bad news in the note. I did not want to read it.

"Caroline Gardiner died with it in her pocket."

"What's it about?"

"It's addressed to you."

With no small amount of trepidation, I gingerly turned over the plastic bag and read the note written on a piece of hotel stationary. *St. James, find my killer* was scrawled across the page.

Praise for St. James Investigates

Aggie St. James is a smart, wise-cracking addition to the pantheon of private-investigator heroines. I loved this book. Inez Phillips brings a welcome fresh voice to the crime novel genre.

~Marcia Preston, Mary Higgins Clark Award winner
for *Song of the Bones*

~*~

Aggie St. James is a private detective with a sense of humor, a knack for getting herself in and out of trouble, and a cat with a personality. *St. James Investigates* is a fast and fun read.

~Linda Shelby, author of *A Splinter in Time*

~*~

There's a new mystery writer in town. Nancy Drew has grown up and now she's Aggie St. James with an irresistible mix of humor and mystery.

~John T. Biggs *Writer's Digest* Grand
Prize Winner

St. James Investigates

by

Inez B. Phillips

St. James Investigates

Contact Information: info@thewildrosepress.com

Cover Art by *Diana Carlile*

The Wild Rose Press, Inc.
PO Box 708
Adams Basin, NY 14410-0708
Visit us at www.thewildrosepress.com

Publishing History
First Edition, 2022
Trade Paperback ISBN 978-1-5092-4412-6
Digital ISBN 978-1-5092-4413-3

Published in the United States of America

Dedication

To all of the people along the way who helped me
become a better writer

Acknowledgments

Thanks to Wendy, Brian, and the rest of my family for encouraging me to keep writing.

A special thank you to the Tuesday Morning Critique Group: Linda, Rakell, Marcia, and John—you are the best.

Chapter 1

The mid-afternoon fog shrouded the sun as the city ground to a halt. The dingy, gray mist swirled outside my fourth-floor window obscuring my view of the Golden Gate Bridge. On a clear day, if I looked to the west, I could just see the east end of it. Since nothing exciting had happened all day, I thought about closing the office and getting an early start in the traffic jam.

The opening notes of "Death and Transfiguration" interrupted the direction of my thoughts. Fumbling through my purse for the phone, I noted the name of an uptown hotel before I clicked it on. I heard a whispered plea for help before the connection broke off.

I received a lot of nuisance calls, but this one bothered me. Usually there were bar sounds or giggling in the background. The unmistakable sound of desperation warned me that this probably wasn't just another crackpot trying to hassle a private investigator. I shrugged into my windbreaker and climbed onto a pair of faux alligator heels. I slammed out of the office and caught the elevator just before the door closed.

The sleazy hotel was about three blocks from my office. I took one look at the cars lined up bumper to bumper and decided the walk would do me good.

Age and pollution blackened the bricks of the Bayside Residence Hotel. It looked like any other place built fifty years ago and left to molder undeterred by care or maintenance. The lobby with its shabby chairs and stained wallpaper mirrored the exterior.

"I received a call from a woman that originated from this hotel." I explained to the desk clerk. "Do you have any women here who might be in distress?"

He put his racing form aside and cleared his throat. "The only woman checked in is in Room 214."

"Do you have her name?"

"Let me look," he said reaching for the dog-eared register. "It says here she's Jane Johnson."

"Did she have any identification?"

He dismissed me with a look of disgust and shook his head. He rattled the racing form, ran his finger down a marked-up column a couple of times before marking another one.

The elevator could have been the first one installed by Otis and the stairs didn't look much safer. I opted to walk up since the stairs wouldn't get stuck between floors. I might need running room if I bumped into any two or four-legged rats.

Locating the room number 214 was easy, but not knowing who or what waited behind the door, made me hesitate. I leaned against the wall, fondled my Smith and Wesson with one hand and rapped on the door with the other.

"Who's there?" a high-pitched voice filtered through the flimsy door.

"Aggie St. James," I called loudly. "I'm with St. James Investigations."

The safety chain rattled, then the door inched open and a shaky voice beckoned me to enter. Wild auburn hair framed her tear-blotched face. My first impression was that she was out of place.

Life hadn't been kind to her. Cleaning and pressing failed to disguise the threadbare cuffs or alter the style of her clothes. Her chain-store shoes were scuffed with the left one missing the plastic beading from the toe.

She perched on the edge of the bed, head bowed, speaking so softly that I had to lean close to hear her. Caroline Rand Gardiner said she had closed her eyes and picked my name out of the directory.

"Someone's trying to kill me," she murmured, a tear slipped down her cheek.

"Why didn't you go to the police?" I hoped to avoid more tears.

"They won't help until a crime's been committed." She tugged at the hem of her skirt, forcing it down at least a half an inch. "They told me I was imagining things."

I sat in a stained plastic chair and asked her to tell me what happened.

"The brakes on my car failed this morning and I had to steer into a ditch to keep from running into the back of a huge truck."

"That could've just been an accident," I suggested. "What makes you think it was attempted murder?"

"There's been a lot of things happening since K.K. died last month." She tucked a wayward strand of fiery hair behind her left ear.

"K.K.?" I asked. "Was that a friend of yours?"

"Oh, no." She seemed to come to life for the first time since I walked through the door. "I got K.K. when he was just a baby."

"What did K.K. die of?"

"The vet said he was poisoned, but I don't see how that was possible because we always shared our food

3

and I didn't die." She shook her head and uttered another deep, breathy sigh.

"I take it that K.K. was a pet of some kind." The police were on the right track. She sounded like a nut with a good imagination. "Did the vet say how K.K. ingested the poison?" I thought I would play along and see just how far this would go before we got to the punch line.

"It was in our coffee."

"K.K. drank coffee?" Maybe she had a straitjacket hanging in the closet.

"Every morning since he was a tiny kitten, we each had a cup. K.K.—I called him that because he was such a cute little kitten—liked his coffee with two spoons of sugar and a half a cup of cream and I had mine black." A wistful smile lit her face as if she were remembering better times.

"Then you didn't actually drink out of the same cup?"

"Never." She straightened up and took on the air of a school teacher trying to explain restroom rules to a messy little boy without using a single word he could understand. "People have many more germs than kittens. It's always better for the kitty to eat first. It's healthier that way. Besides K.K. only liked the pink china and I used the bone white."

"Where did the poison come from?" This was one of those conversations that seemed to be going nowhere and taking forever to get there.

"It was in the sugar bowl."

"Did you have it analyzed?"

"No, but I showed it to Ames and he said it looked and tasted like arsenic."

"Ames?"

"You could call Ames a butler, but I thought of him as a friend."

Fine china, a butler, and threadbare clothes didn't come together for me. I had the distinct feeling that I knew exactly what a schizophrenic's world looked like.

"Does Ames agree that someone was trying to kill you and got the cat instead?"

"I don't know." She paused long enough to cross her legs. "He left the next day and I haven't seen him since."

Exit one figment of her imagination. "Is there anything other than a dead cat to make you believe that someone is trying to kill you?"

"When I got home from shopping last Friday the house smelled like gas. Someone blew out the pilot lights and turned the burners on and then, Saturday, while I was walking along Market Street, someone tried to shove me in front of a bus."

"Did you see anyone you knew on the street?"

"By the time I got up, there wasn't anyone around."

She seemed to run down like an old clock. Ms. Gardiner slumped so low that she looked like she might slide right onto the floor.

"Why do you think someone's trying to kill you?" I wasn't sure why but I felt like I was in the middle of a B-grade science fiction film festival. Either the police were right about her imagination or whoever was trying to kill her had the worst luck in the world.

"Well, some of my husband's cousins and his brother seemed to be upset the last time I saw them," she muttered after a long pause. "And then there was the woman who claimed my husband was the father of her twins, and the people who wanted to sue us because our backyard slid into their front yard after our sprinkler system broke while we were on our first honeymoon, and then there's the housekeeper I fired for putting food in the attic." Ms. Gardiner just looked at me and shrugged, her voice fading away.

With that list I hardly knew where to start. "Has your husband had any near misses?"

The predictable tears I dreaded started to fall. I handed her a packet of tissues from my pocket and went over to stare out the window. Maybe, I thought, by the time the five o'clock traffic cleared, her waterworks might have dried up.

I turned at the sound of a wheezing cough in time to see her repairing her face. The compact she held in front of the damages had enough jewels in it to fund at least six of my most expensive fantasies. It's too bad she hadn't spent part of the money on some decent clothes and a better hotel.

She cleared her throat. "I'm sorry," she said just loudly enough to be heard across the room. "I'm usually in better control." She tucked the compact into a Coach handbag.

I really wanted to ask about the purse and compact. Even with her shabby clothes perhaps she could afford my fees. Not wanting to change the subject, I waited for her to go on. With a story like hers, it was hard to decide what to ask next.

"My Ronald died a month ago. He died of a heart attack while we were on our second honeymoon," she blubbered. "It was so sad. We were in the middle of playing Cobra and Mongoose when the doorbell rang. I heard this really loud hiss and then a crash when Ronald fell into the aspidistra."

"Aspi...what?" It took me a while but it occurred to me that I knew a homicide detective from the Park Precinct who was going to pay for this one. I like a joke as well as the next person, but pointing this fruitcake in my direction was going too far.

"As-pi-dis-tra," she enunciated slowly. "It was a large, green plant in the entry way, right beside the table where the room service people put the trays."

"What made the hissing sound?" I asked, trying to keep a straight face. I figured that I'd stay for the end of the joke.

"That's what I asked the police when they came to investigate Ronald's death, but they just kept laughing about the size of the aspidistra or something. I never could understand what they meant." Ms. Gardiner started rubbing her arms as if she were trying to restore her circulation. She looked so confused and distraught that I began to doubt my original assessment.

"Where were you when Ronald fell into the foliage?"

"I was in the bathroom."

"I meant, where was the motel where you and Ronald were honeymooning?"

"New Mexico about fifteen miles from the Arizona border. I think it was called the Bates Motel."

I stood up and pulled on my jacket, draped a scarf around my neck. Reaching for the door, I turned to look at her one more time. I didn't want to forget that face in case Liam Alexander decided to trot her out again in another of his not-so-funny practical jokes.

"Where you going?" She stood up abruptly, a

surprised look on her face.

"Tell your cop friend that he came close this time. It's too bad you threw in the hissing aspidistra and the Bates Motel. You almost had me believing you." I shook my head as I pulled the door shut behind me.

Chapter 2

The phone jangled, destroying the dream of my favorite meal of crab legs and baked Alaska. As the vision disappeared, I grabbed the phone and squinted at the numbers on the clock. It was four o'clock, not even the crack of dawn. Rumbling static on the line sounded like a nightmare with a toothache. I turned the phone over in time to hear Liam Alexander make slighting references about my family, sexual preferences, and various members of the animal kingdom.

"Whatdoyawant?" I coughed and tried to clear the morning phlegm. Liam paused in his invective just long enough for me to quit hacking and then he started in on my habits.

"If you'd quit living like a rat in a toxic waste dump, you wouldn't make me sick to my stomach every time I have to—"

I pushed the phone under the pillow and headed for the bathroom. No matter how long it took for me to get back, he wouldn't be finished with his diatribe. One night I left it on the floor and went back to sleep. He was still after me when the alarm went off a half hour later.

Liam and I grew up on the same block in Mission District. I spent more time with his family than I did with my own. Every time my stepfather came home drunk and started hitting my mom, I'd climb out the bathroom window and head over to Liam's. When my mother died from a skull fracture, I was practically living in his closet. His mom decided to find out how a stick like Liam could eat enough for three and never gain an ounce. She found me, called the social welfare people, and took me in legally. I was glad to get out of the closet, but it sure has cost me a lot. I've never figured out how to say no to Liam.

I picked up the phone and grunted loud enough to get him to pause his monologue. Liam never called me in the middle of the night to check on my health.

"Do you know a Caroline Gardiner?" he asked without preamble.

"You know more about her than I do."

"What makes you jump to that conclusion?"

"That business in the hotel had your fingerprints all over it," I growled. "You could call and gloat at a more respectable hour."

"I should've let you out of the closet more often—you spent too much time sniffing old gym shoes and dirty underwear. Meet me at Bailey's in thirty minutes or I'll come over and slam a window on your fingers for old times' sake."

I could gauge the urgency of the message by how much noise he made hanging up the phone. This time it was so loud he almost took my head off.

Stepping out of my apartment building into the blinding rain made me hope that this might be the end of my debt to Liam. The rain washed the stink of traffic out of the air and drove the night people into shelters and doorways. The eyes still followed me, but the rain insulated me from their bitter destitution. I just have to run into one of those human derelicts to remember how grateful I am that Liam's mother kept me from becoming one of them.

The smell of fresh-brewed coffee and frying bacon greeted me as I stumbled into Bailey's. It had been an institution in the neighborhood for years. The original Bailey had retired to Florida and now his granddaughter Marlene was in charge. She put a mug of coffee in my outstretched hand and pointed me toward the table closest to the kitchen. Liam and his partner, the one I called the Mediterranean flatfoot, were inhaling their food. They both looked like they were hoping for a reason to see if their bullets worked.

My food beat me to the table. I grimaced at Marlene and she just crossed her eyes. Marlene grew up in the old neighborhood and knew how to read Liam almost as well as I could. She wasn't about to stick around to see what was eating at him this time.

"It's about time you dragged your worthless ass out of bed," Liam snarled into his coffee mug. "I hope your brain's working better now than it was the last time I talked to you."

"If you learned a few manners, we wouldn't have to go through this every time you need the help of an expert." I like to remind him that I made detective before I left the force. It took him another two years to get his gold shield.

Max Ciardi, his partner, glared at me across the table. "Pretty manners aren't going to make your life any easier when we get through sending you up on a murder rap."

"Blow it out your—"

"All right," interrupted Liam. "This is bad enough

without you two starting up again."

Liam signaled for a refill and pulled a plastic evidence bag out of his notebook. There was a crumpled piece of paper in it. "Can you explain this?"

It was a scrap torn from the yellow pages. Several private investigators' names were underlined but mine had a great big circle around the number. I handed it back to him and dug into my eggs. "Looks like my name," I mumbled. "Where do you suppose she found a phone book?"

"Who cares about the phone book," Max said around a mouthful of eggs. "Can you tell us why we found it wadded up in a dead woman's pocket?"

"Maybe she needed more help than you were able to give her," I reached for the Tabasco. The eggs at Bailey's had only one thing going for them—they were yellow.

Liam put his hand on Ciardi's shoulder to stop him from coming all the way out of his chair. "Now that you've got that out of your system, what can you tell us about the woman?"

"What woman?" I chugged a glass of water trying to neutralize the hot sauce.

"Caroline Rand Gardiner."

"You know her better than I do." I fanned the last of the hot sauce. "I'm having a hard time figuring out why you dragged me out of bed in the middle of night just to rehash one of your sophomoric jokes." I threw some money on the table and reached for my raincoat.

"We found her dead and your fingerprints were in her hotel room."

Liam's words stopped me cold. I hadn't heard him use that tone since his mother died in a hit-and-run with a drunk. I had to cold cock him to stop him from killing that guy.

"She was alive and sniffling when I left her this afternoon," I said, dropping back into the empty chair.

"What makes you think Liam had anything to do with her?" growled Ciardi.

I tried for a long time to figure out how to tell what kind of mood Max was in from the sound of his voice. I even asked Liam and he told me not to worry about it—just assume he was always ready to kill and you'd be about right.

"It's hard to say whether it was the Bates Motel or the big aspidistra." I finished my coffee and slammed the cup down. "One thing about it, she sure had me going for a while, especially her crying. I don't think I've ever seen anyone who could shed as many tears at one time as she did yesterday afternoon."

Liam leaned back in his chair and shook his head. "I've got the feeling that there are two conversations going on here. Humor me, tell me what I did that was so funny."

"You didn't arrange for that woman to call me and try to hire me to find out who was trying to kill her?" Liam might be a practical joker and my biggest critic, but I knew he wouldn't lie with me looking him in the face.

He shook his head and signaled for some more coffee. Marlene refilled our mugs and flipped a business card in front of Ciardi.

Ciardi glanced at it and handed it back. "Tell her to get lost."

"Are you sure?" Marlene batted her eyes at him and beat it back to the cash register. Teasing Ciardi about collecting business cards was risky if not completely dangerous. I never understood why but his iron-jawed, swarthy face appealed to women. It didn't seem to matter whether they were old, young, married, single, rich, or poor. He always collected a half a handful of cards and phone numbers every time he walked through a restaurant or bar. Ciardi glowered as Marlene blew him a kiss. She had known him long enough to know that his pretty face masked a personality that had a lot in common with a train wreck.

"Why don't you tell us about the Gardiner woman so we can get out of here?" Max snapped.

I gave them a rundown on what had happened at the Bayside Hotel yesterday afternoon. Then I had a few questions of my own.

"Why is an uptown bag lady with a diamond compact of interest to you? I thought you only investigated the very best."

"Have you heard of Gardiner Electronics?" asked Liam.

Who hadn't heard of the company? They had reportedly developed a process for reusing nuclear waste water in the production of electricity. People from all over the world were pounding on their door hoping for a piece of the action.

"Mrs. Caroline Rand Gardiner held controlling interest in the company due to the untimely demise of her husband, the founder and genius behind the family fortune." Ciardi enunciated every word carefully in case my hearing had failed.

"Do the brother and cousins she mentioned stand to gain from her death?"

"If the annual stockholders' reports can be

believed, the family holdings are worth seven hundred million dollars, give or take a few." Liam shuffled through his notes. "Ronald Gardiner, the C.E.O., owned sixty-one percent of the stock while various investors split the other thirty-nine. We haven't had a chance to check on a will yet."

"Did Caroline and Ronald have any children?" I pictured a mental list of suspects that kept growing.

"No." Put in Ciardi. "She was his secretary for exactly one week before they hustled off to Las Vegas and got married."

"That must have been a surprise to all." I snatched a piece of Ciardi's bacon.

Max moved his plate out of my reach. "Ronald Gardiner was fifty-eight when they got married. His family was ready to spend all of their assets to get him declared incompetent for marrying someone thirty-five years younger than he was."

"Did it work?"

"Gardiner got wind of what they were trying to do and fired the lot of them just before he and Caroline went on their second honeymoon which, incidentally, began one week after the first one ended."

"That certainly explains the clothes." I shook my head in disbelief. "She hadn't been out of bed long enough to shop. Maybe that's why they were playing Mongoose and Cobra. They didn't have enough time to buy any leather goods."

"What in the hell are you talking about?" snapped Ciardi.

"I didn't ask," I fought with the sleeve of my raincoat. "I thought maybe it was something you liked to play with your many admirers. How about explaining it to me sometime?" I stood up and buttoned my coat. "I'm out of here. This is no concern of mine."

"What makes you think that?" Liam bared enough teeth to make a shark jealous. A stranger might have thought he was smiling, but I knew better. He was snickering up his sleeve and, whatever it was, the joke was on me.

"No client, no money, no case." I tossed back at him. "I don't do charity work."

"I think this is yours." He held an evidence bag with an envelope in it between his forefinger and thumb. My name was scrawled in purple curlicue letters across the envelope. The only other mark was the Bayside Hotel logo. A piece of note paper was in another evidence bag.

"What are those?"

"An envelope and letter."

"Where did you find them?" That envelope had all the charm of a spitting python. I could sense bad news in the note. I did not want to read it.

"Caroline Gardiner died with it in her pocket."

"What's it about?"

"It's addressed to you."

With no small amount of trepidation, I gingerly turned over the plastic bag and read the note written on a piece of hotel stationary. *St. James, find my killer* was scrawled across the page. She added the name of a law firm to contact if I needed more money. Liam held up a third envelope with several hundred-dollar bills in it.

****

Caroline Rand Gardiner died of gunshot wounds to the chest and abdomen. No signs of forcible entry or a struggle were found in the room. The small caliber slugs were being checked by the lab and, from the amount of noise the desk clerk heard, a silencer was not used. The police ran down every witness who might have been in the hotel at the time but, as usual, they were either blind or deaf or both. They saw and heard nothing and most of them disappeared without a trace immediately after the police finished with them.

Liam and Ciardi took me over to the room where she died and walked me through my story again. Her personal effects were at the crime lab so there wasn't much to see except blood stains on the wall and floor.

"Where are you going to start looking?" Liam asked as we left the hotel.

"First, I'm going to get some sleep. Then I'm going to your office and read your reports."

"Not on your life," snapped Ciardi. "We aren't running an information service for over-paid PIs. If you want to read reports, go write some." He jammed on his hat and stalked down the street toward their unmarked car.

"Do you think you can quit baiting Max just long enough for me to retire before he throttles you? I don't want to have to explain to a judge why it was justifiable homicide."

"Liam, you know I love you like a brother and I'd do almost anything for you, but if I didn't give him a hard time, he'd have nothing to look forward to except those card-toting ladies. I think he hates them even more than he hates me." I patted Liam on the arm in mock sympathy. "Why don't you trade him in on a Gila monster—your job will be safer and you'll enjoy your work a lot more."

Chapter 3

I went back to my apartment and tried to take up where I left off. I dozed fitfully, dreaming of blood, relatives, and business cards with Ciardi's mug floating over them. After about an hour I gave up and stumbled out of bed.

I switched on the coffee maker and started my list of things to do and people to see. It always helped to write them down and stare at them for a while. It had never helped me solve a case, but it gave me something to hold when I spoke with my clients. A well-used notebook made them think I was onto something important. Except in this case, everyone I needed to talk to was dead.

With so many people having unkind feelings toward Ronald and Caroline, it was hard to tell just where to start. The people with the sliding lawn were the least likely to commit murder. If I were they, I'd set fire to the Gardiner's house and cheer while it burned. The woman with the paternity suit probably wouldn't kill the prospective father. That'd be a little too much like killing the goose with the golden eggs, or sperm in this case. The death of Ronald Gardiner seemed to be as good a place to start as any.

The Bates Motel that Caroline told me about may not have been the site of Anthony Perkins's finest hour, but it was the final scene in the Ronald and Caroline romance. She said it was located just east of the Arizona border on I-40.

****

The New Mexico Tourist Bureau told me the only motel in the state that sounded like Bates was the Bayett near the Wingate offramp. I flew into the Holbrook Municipal Airport and rented a Jeep with a GPS. I took a paper map as a backup.

When I was a teenager my grandparents decided I needed to see the Wild West through the bug-splattered windows of their old minivan. Embarrassed by the faded astrological signs and psychedelic swirls painted on the sides of the van, I spent most of the trip slumped in the back reading a book. When forced to get out to look at every historic marker and roadside attraction we came to, I hid behind the largest sunglasses I could find.

This time I sailed past the Painted Desert and the Petrified Forest. Stopping by the Zuni reservation for a pot or two was off the agenda, too. I remembered having to climb out and look at Church Rock which turned out to be a huge rock formation of religious significance to one of the tribes in the area. The trip through the Southwest seemed to take forever. And so did my fifteenth summer.

I entertained myself by estimating the distance to the next hill and checking my answer. Wingate was a wide spot in the road. So small they didn't list population on the *Welcome to the Wingate* sign.

I located a small adobe building with a faded Sheriff sign nailed over the door. The door squeaked when I pushed it open. The office needed a good dusting and a general makeover. The paint was peeling and the wanted posters were yellow with age. A man in khakis and a t-shirt that said POLICE eyed me over a tattered copy of Penthouse.

I held out my credentials. "Where can I find information about the death of Ronald Gardener at the Bayett Motel?"

He dropped his feet to the floor and peered at my license over the desk, then pointed at another door without lowering his magazine. "Juan Baca can help you."

Baca sat at a table in a room that looked more like a closet than a detective's office. With a passing glance at my P.I. ticket, he handed me a thin file with one page detailing the police investigation and a half page set forth the autopsy findings. It was the shortest coroner's report in history. The report indicated that he died of a heart attack. Although the widow agreed to an autopsy, I couldn't find the toxicology report or any indication that he had been cut open.

"Why weren't any tests run for poison or other foreign substances?" I asked Baca after I finished reading the file.

Baca, acting like the department Lothario, flashed a smile that revealed about forty pearly-white teeth and took the file out of my hand. Posing himself on the corner of the table that served as a desk, he gave me a look that would've offended every feminist in North America.

"Now just why would you want to know a thing like that?" he asked, baring his perfect teeth again. He looked me up and down then focused on my breasts.

"Toxicology is usually a part of an autopsy," I replied, trying not to let his patronizing attitude get to me. "I'd simply like to know why it wasn't done."

"The coroner decided that the cause of death was self-evident and it cut costs for the county." He gave me a wink when he mentioned saving money. It was obvious his respect for women never got beyond the bedroom door.

"Mrs. Gardiner reported hearing a hissing sound before he fell. Did the investigating officers find an explanation for this?"

Baca's face closed up and he stood abruptly. "Where'd you hear that?" The friendly, good cop had disappeared.

I wasn't willing to share anything with this lecherous paper-pusher. "May I speak to the officers who answered the call?"

He dropped the folder onto the table and yelled at the man on the desk. "Samuels, escort Ms. St. James to the street." He gestured toward the door with his head. "I'm required by law to let you review the police report, but I won't permit you to grill any of our officers. The investigation was thorough and we don't need some big-city private eye coming in here and saying we don't know what we're doing."

By the time he finished, Samuels had a death grip on my arm and I was halfway out of the building. "Thanks for your cooperation," was the only thing I had time to say before he slammed the door.

I found the Bayett Motor Inn, a respectable-looking establishment just off I-40. It could've passed for a normal mom-and-pop operation except for the HOURLY and DAY RATES sign. It wasn't the nicest motel I have ever seen nor was it the shabbiest.

A bell chimed as I entered the motel office. A middle-aged woman came in from the backroom. "May I help you?" She was dressed in baggy Bermuda shorts and a yellow striped shirt with the Bayett logo on the sleeve. I couldn't see her feet, but I heard the tell-tale slap of flipflops every time she moved.

"Yes." I held out my credentials. "Did a Ronald Gardiner stay here recently?"

"Um." She looked at me warily. "Why do you ask?"

"His wife wants me to make inquiries." I was reluctant to give her the specifics.

"Why don't you ask her about his stay?"

"She's unavailable right now." I used to cross my fingers when I told a lie, but I outgrew the habit. "Is the room they stayed in vacant?"

"Yes. Do you want it?"

Eighty dollars bought me one night in the same room where the Gardiners spent their last joyful hours. It was the generic motel room with two exceptions—an oversized bed and a damaged aspidistra. The walls were a dun color and the carpet could have hidden evidence of numerous crimes. Nothing would show on that brown-gray-puce color.

A bellboy named Hiram hustled me to the room. Hustled might be too strong a word for his pace. Hiram moved like he and God had played on the same high school football team. He wore a suit that had once been black, but it had faded to a sooty gray. His shirt could have used a good bleaching. He stood around to see if the room met with my approval and he probably would've taken off sooner if I'd been a little faster with the tip.

I asked him what happened to the plant. He gave me a pained expression and did an arthritic shuffle around my question. The only thing he said that made sense was that something fell on it.

"No kidding." I handed him a dollar.

He turned it over, snapped it a couple of times, and held it up to the light. This was a time-honored act guaranteed to make the tipper feel cheap. It didn't work.

"If you want to see that guy's big brother, you're going to have to tell me something I don't already know about that plant." I spoke with just enough sarcasm to get his interest. I pulled a twenty out of my bag and held it out for him to see.

"I'm not sure what you know," he muttered. Every hotel in the world went to heroic efforts to deny that a death had taken place in one of their rooms. This motel was no different.

"I know that room service didn't drop a tray on it," I snapped. My patience is short on the best of days and today it was almost nonexistent. "Someone died in this room and I want the details."

The old man heaved his shoulders and let out an extended wheeze. "Uh," he began. His voice sounded like it was coming from the far end of a long tunnel. "About a month ago this man and woman checked in saying they were married and on their second honeymoon. We didn't pay a lot of attention because everybody says they're honeymooning."

He paused in his narration just long enough to settle himself in the only chair in the room. His joints cracked and the chair creaked. It was a toss-up as to which was louder.

"The only thing that I could see different about them was that they had a couple of suitcases. A lot of people checking in here seem to only have a sack from the pharmacy across the road and smarmy looks on their faces." He gave me a wink that was supposed to explain a lot and continued. "They'd been here for almost a week without ever leaving the room."

This certainly fit with everything I'd heard about the Gardiners. "What did they eat?"

"We...ll," he managed to stretch the word to at least three syllables. "They got deliveries from about every take-out joint from here to Gallop. The rest of the time they called room service."

"Did you deliver for room service?"

"Mostly...except on my day off and then Mavis Owens took care of it." He sounded like he was beginning to run down so I pulled another twenty out of my pocket and held it in my hand.

"Did you talk to either of them when you delivered their meals?"

He pursed his lips and shook his head. "Nope," he said with a great air of finality. "Never saw either one of them."

"How was that possible?" I looked around the room. "What did they do? Hide under the bed?"

"Can't rightly say." He stroked an imaginary beard. "I think they stayed mostly in the bathroom or at least that's how it sounded."

"Are you sure they were even in here?"

"Yup," he said without hesitation. "When Mavis noticed that they never left the room and the maid reported that they wouldn't let her in to change the sheets, we all started a betting pool on when they'd leave. Nobody left this room all week and you can bet your bottom dollar on it."

In a motel where people came and went at all hours of the day and night, it must have been quite a treat to have someone hibernating. "Can you tell me who else was in on the watch?"

"There's just Mavis and me and Adam Franklin, the night man, and Pepita who does most of the cooking."

"Did you ever see anyone other than delivery people go into the room?"

He started looking hazy again. It was a look I had come to recognize over the years. He was like a parking meter; he only ran for so long then you had to pour more money into him. I dug for another twenty and added it to the two in my hand. Like magic, the old man perked up and started talking again.

"The night Mr. Gardiner died, there was a black car parked in front of the room for a little while." He had a faraway look in his eyes like he was trying to recall a fleeting memory of his youth. "I watched it for a while, but the fog was so thick that I really couldn't make out anything about the driver. I got a call from A-201 for a bucket of ice and when I got back, that car was gone."

"Did you hear anything unusual?"

"Nope." He shook his head slowly. "There wasn't a thing going on."

I held out the three twenties to him. He started to take them, but I held them just beyond of his reach. "One more thing, did you tell the police about the black car?"

"Nope."

"Why?"

"They didn't ask."

Chapter 4

New Mexico was a disappointment. I found out very little other than the police weren't excited about helping me and the strange black car remained a mystery. I caught the red-eye back to San Francisco. I prefer early morning flights when almost everyone on the plane is awake. At night there always seems to be a man seated near me who divides his time between snoring and passing gas. Trying to go up the aisle to the tiny restroom requires climbing over feet and dodging heads hanging in the aisle. Flying at night is a precursor of hell.

I called Liam Alexander and asked him to meet me at the airport. He wasn't thrilled, but he owed me after getting me out of bed the night of the murder.

I waited beside the line of taxis watching my fellow passengers disperse. A stocky, little man with a nose ring and a snake tattoo around his neck sidled up to me and offered to share a cab. He was dressed in California chic: board shorts topped with a purple wife-beater shirt and flip-flops.

"Thank you." I stepped back a pace. "I have a ride coming."

He shrugged and moved back into the line of people waiting for taxicabs.

I met a lot of people here in California who would

stand out in any other part of the world. Here, they just blend in. I was watching him climb into a taxi with a couple of elderly women when Liam showed up.

"Come on, I'm parked in a loading zone."

I had to take an occasional running step to keep up with him. I jumped in the car half a heartbeat before he peeled away from the curb.

"Was it worth the trip?" He began without so much as a hello.

"I'm so happy you were able to meet me and I really appreciate the ride home." I smiled up at him. "That's a beautiful silk shirt you're wearing." I ran my hand across his chest and patted his stomach a couple of times.

"Cut the crap." He pushed my hand away. "Keep your hands off the shirt." He always did wake up nasty, even when I knocked on his window at three in the morning.

"Did you put this on for someone special or are you dressing better for the sandman?" I snickered. I had given him the vermilion silk pajamas when he was hospitalized with a bullet wound. He hadn't expressed a lot of appreciation then either.

"Oh, shut up," he said. "It was the only clean shirt I could find."

Liam wove through the airport traffic like a Formula One driver trying to qualify for the French Grand Prix. We were on the freeway headed north before I felt it was safe to talk to him about my trip to New Mexico.

"The only thing I learned was that Caroline and Ronald had incredible staying power." I laughed, as Liam leaned on the horn to get a slow-moving Chevy out of the way. "They didn't even leave the room for food."

"That is not exactly newsworthy," Liam said.

"There's a coroner's report without an autopsy, a very sensitive police sergeant, and an unidentified black car outside the Gardiner's room just before he died." I summed up the miserable trip in as few words as possible. The unabridged version wouldn't have taken much longer.

"What did the police reports say about the black car?"

"Nothing." I rolled down the window. I had missed the sweet smell of partially burned diesel fuel and exhaust fumes. "The motel mafia watched the Gardiner's room all week for signs of life. They only answered the questions they were asked . . ."

"...and no one asked about the car." Liam supplied the ending. You might get the idea that he can read my mind and maybe he can to a certain extent. "Did it cost a lot to get the motel mafia to talk?"

"Not a lot." I watched him negotiate the off ramp and turn toward his condo. "Is there a reason why you're taking me home with you?"

"Hobo needs his box cleaned," he muttered.

I have a fondness for stray cats, maybe because I was one myself. When I found one shivering on the street, I would take it in until I could locate a home for it. Liam happened by the day I had picked up a taffy-colored kitten that just matched his couch. For three years I have had to go over and change the litter for them. Liam won't and the cat can't.

His condo was on the first floor of a converted warehouse. It boasted a bedroom separated from the rest of the living space by a bunch of over-grown weeds he refers to as greenery. A couple of empty bird cages that hung from the ceiling were hidden among the foliage. Hobo ate the birds long ago and now uses the cages for batting practice.

The litter box was three weeks past filthy. When I finally finished cleaning the mess and brushed Hobo's fur until it stood out like a mall groupie's spike, I looked around for Liam. Following the wheezing buzz, I found him stretched out at an angle across the bed, his clothes in a pile on the floor. I threw a quilt over him and headed for the bathroom.

The shower, patterned after those added to old European hotel rooms to please the American tourists, featured a tiled floor with a circular curtain to keep the water from spraying all over the room. He had the devil's own time trying to get the water to run down the drain instead of into the closet. He solved the problem by adding a three-inch high toe-killing brick edge around the tiles.

I grabbed my foot and hopped around swearing at Liam's brick work. His only reaction was to snort and roll over. Although I was tempted to throw water on him, I didn't want to listen to another lecture about my ancestors and their numerous faults.

By the time I used all the hot water, my toe had turned pale blue and only hurt when it touched the floor. I dried off with the only towel Liam owned and hung it up carefully so it would be dry when he needed it.

Liam never owned more than one towel. He reasoned that he could only use one at a time and how could it get dirty if it was only used to dry off a clean body. Every time I referred to his housekeeping tendencies, he offered to let me do it if I thought he needed to improve. I've learned to keep my mouth shut and let his warped ideas about cleanliness fester without my interference.

I pulled on a Forty-niners t-shirt and climbed into bed. With Liam still lying across the middle, I had to crawl in at an angle. I yanked a blanket from under him and got as comfortable as possible. Sleeping in the leftover space beat trying to rest on his four-and-a-half-foot couch.

Tiny dust bunnies and bits of cat fur danced in the sunlight as a deep-throated rumble vibrated my pillow and a heavy weight lay across my stomach. I tried to tug my hair out from under the cat while Liam tightened his grip and snuggled against my back.

"Lie still." He threw one leg over mine and caressed the thin cotton of my night shirt.

"Liam." I whispered through parched lips. "Liam, it's me, Aggie." I tried to squirm of out his grasp.

He rolled me over and buried his face between my neck and shoulder. "Don't do it, Mandy." He shifted slightly to nuzzle one ear. "I love you, babe."

I worked one hand free and cupped his chin, forcing his head up until he faced me. "Liam," I called softly. "Liam, wake up. It's me, Aggie."

Liam hadn't mentioned Mandy for years and he'd never mistaken me for her. Something happened while I was in New Mexico—something that dredged up the old memories.

"Mandy," he breathed in my ear. "Mandy, I can't live without you." He tried to break my grip on his chin, his knee forcing my legs apart. I freed my other hand and pinched his nose until he gasped for air.

"Liam," I said louder. "Liam, Mandy's gone."

His eyes snapped open and he took a great gulp of air. Chagrin quickly replaced the confusion in his glazed eyes. "I'm sorry, Aggie. I guess I was having a nightmare." He buried his face in my hair and wrapped both arms tightly around me, rocking back and forth as if trying to expel a ghost.

"I'd be flattered if this was my doing, but since it isn't, would you mind getting off me?" I groaned. "I'm not crazy about being squashed when there is nothing in it for me."

Liam rolled over with me in his arms until I was lying on top of him. "Let me hold you a little longer," he muttered against my neck, encircling me in a cocoon of arms and legs.

He didn't have to explain. I knew what soul-killing loneliness can do to you. Liam held me for days while David lay in intensive care dying by inches. A stray bullet from a liquor store robbery ended our two-year marriage. David had lavished me with a love I never thought possible. Liam held me long enough to keep me from crawling into the grave with him.

Long minutes later, his grip loosened and I could feel him relax. "What happened while I was gone?" I asked as I tried to slide over onto the mattress. He cradled my head on his shoulder and turned just enough for me to stretch out on the cool muslin sheets. I could feel his heart speed up as he paused before answering my question.

"The Ashworth officials in Redding called yesterday." His voice broke and he tightened his grip on me. "Mandy tried to hang herself then escaped from the prison ward in the hospital. They think she's headed this way."

"Do you think she'll try for you again?" I asked.

"Mandy's psychiatrist said that her delusions were becoming more pronounced." Liam tried to clear the rest of the morning grit out of his throat. "She's decided that you helped me arrange the accident and she began including you in her threats about two years ago."

"What's she threatening this time?" I raised up on one elbow and brushed a lock of hair off his forehead.

"She's planning to kill us.

Liam and Mandy were grade school sweethearts who lived the American dream. He played quarterback on the high school football team and she was the head cheerleader who lived around the corner. Their story, destined for a happily-after ending, got sidetracked when Mandy missed a curve on Highway 101.

The mechanics reassembled the MG Midget and the doctors pieced her back together. They both looked as if they were in mint condition, but neither one of them performed right again. The car kept pulling to the left and Mandy blamed Liam for the accident.

"Has she contacted you yet?" I asked, gathering up my clothes.

"There were a couple of hang-ups on the machine yesterday but no messages," he mumbled on his way to the shower.

The sound of running water kept me from asking any more questions so I pulled on my clothes and headed for the coffee pot. Hobo wrapped himself around my legs and informed me that he expected to be fed first.

I gave the cat some dry food and poured a bowl of

cereal for myself. Liam only bought the low-cholesterol-unsweetened-ultra-high-fiber-tasteless generic stuff that looked a lot like cat food and smells worse than mildewed peanut butter. Every time I had to eat it, I promised myself that I'd bring my own but, I never got around to it.

I had the first spoonful in mid-air when the doorbell rang. It was Ciardi's signature ring, loud and abrasive. Facing Max first thing in the morning was marginally better than eating Liam's cereal.

"What're you doing here?" He snarled on the way to the coffee pot. Max helped himself to a cup and pushed the cat out of the chair at the end of the table.

Hobo's hair bristled as he hissed and took a mighty swing at Max's ankle. Max jumped back like a well-trained ballerina. Then Hobo spun around and headed for the sofa.

"Goddamn cat," Ciardi muttered into his coffee cup.

"I trained him well," I snickered. The Max-and-Hobo show began the first time they met and hasn't changed over the years.

"I thought you were in New Mexico. What'd they do? Run you off?"

Ciardi never looked directly at me. He always looked somewhere over my left shoulder. I think he did it to keep me off balance, but it just made him look slightly cross-eyed.

"They gave me the keys to the city." I tried to down another spoonful of cereal.

"What'd you find out?" He leaned his chair back against the wall.

I couldn't do it. I tried but no part of my digestive

system would cooperate. I poured the rest of the cereal into the garbage disposal and talked about what I learned while the machine screeched and groaned. It sounded like the garbage disposal couldn't stand Liam's cereal either.

"What did you say?" Ciardi asked when the noise died down.

"Which part didn't you understand?" I put the bowl and spoon in the dishwasher.

"Try all of it," Max looked like he wanted to take a swing at me.

"Well, I'm not sure I can make it simple enough for you to understand." I ducked out of the kitchen.

I caught Liam coming out of the shower and told him I was going to grab a cab for the office.

"Take care and call me if you even think Mandy is trying to contact you." He tried to squeeze enough lather out of the can for one last shave.

"Try not to worry." I kissed the tip of my finger and touched his nose.

"How sweet." A rough voice growled behind us.

Liam turned and nodded to Ciardi while I picked up my suitcase and headed for the front door. I handed Max one of my cards and slammed out the door before he had a chance to throw it back at me.

Chapter 5

The early morning traffic had settled down to moderate congestion in front of Liam's condo. I walked a couple of blocks before I could flag down a taxi. I gave the cabbie my office address and leaned back to study my notebook.

The Gardiners were still dead and I wasn't any closer to discovering who killed them. Money was high on the hit parade of motives, but the question was who wanted it badly enough to risk a couple of murder one charges?

I told the cabby to wait while I took my carryon up to my office and exchanged it for the Gardiner file. I ran up the stairs and back so I wouldn't be funding his next vacation. I had him drop me off four blocks away at the garage where I rent a space for my car. Parking was difficult and almost as expensive as renting a car in San Francisco.

The Gardiners lived close to the ocean in the western part of the city. My nav system took me north on Highway 1 to Sloat Boulevard then west toward the Upper Great Highway. I used this route to U Cal San Francisco where I did two semesters before I signed up for the police academy. Going back for a training course last year, I had to get a campus map to find my meeting. I swore the University had jacked up half the buildings and shuffled them just to confuse the alums. Yet the grass was still perfectly flat and green.

The GPS took me past the San Francisco Zoo. My husband and I met in front of the Tropical Rainforest for our first date. One of our favorite pastimes was to enter the zoo in late afternoon and wander around until sunset. Those were memories the bullet couldn't take away.

Following the Great Highway north, I saw the wrought iron arch to the Gardiner property just past Fulton Street. The house, hidden among the trees, was one tower and a moat short of being a castle. I couldn't imagine how much it cost to maintain that pile of bricks. Let alone buy it. The grass needed mowing and the scraggly hedges outlining the estate were in need of an arborist. A boarded-up window and overgrown flower beds spoiled the exterior of the house. I hoped the interior was better maintained.

A tall, dour-faced woman in black slacks and a baggy yellow sweater opened the door. Her gray-streaked hair was pulled back in a knot that was so tight she looked Asian. She smelled like old garlic and didn't look like she bathed with any regularity. The woman tried to block my way into the house, but I dodged around her and stepped into entry way.

"Can you tell me where I can find the butler?" My voice echoed off the bare walls. A couple of dusty tables and an umbrella stand shaped like an elephant's leg were the only furnishings in the enormous entry hall. The housekeeping staff seemed to have been lacking direction for quite a while.

"He ain't here." She spoke with a slight Spanish accent as she gestured toward the open door.

"Where is he?" I wandered in the direction of the double doors. They were slightly ajar and one of them had moved.

"I don't know." She strode around me so she was blocking my way. "If that's all you want, I must ask you to leave."

"Is the owner home?" I watched the door quiver just enough for me to question my eyesight.

"The owner is dead." She stepped toward me trying to force me back toward to front door.

"I want to see whoever is in charge."

"I've been the housekeeper here for more than twenty years." She sniffed like an old hound dog with a runny nose.

Talking with this woman was like pouring water on a sponge. I was putting a lot in and not getting much in return. "I'd like to speak to the person who is paying your wages." I spoke a little louder than necessary thinking that the eavesdropper might want to come out and give her a little help.

"Nobody's paying me." She took another step toward me.

"Then why are you here?"

"Mr. Gardiner told me that he would make up my back wages if I'd stay until the court let him take over." She stood a little taller, peering down her nose at me like the creaky old dragons they used for mothers-in-law in old movies.

"I thought you said Mr. Gardiner was dead." I breathed in and stood a little taller. I refused to allow a housekeeper to intimidate me with cheap breathing tricks.

"Mr. *SAMUEL* Gardiner."

"When does he think he'll take possession?" I asked. "Before or after the murder trial?"

"I have no idea what you're talking about." Her self-confidence seemed to diminish. "Who told you he had anything to do with Mr. Ronald's death?"

"I'm not talking about Mr. Ronald's death." I took stock of the confusion on her face.

"You aren't?" she asked. The color leached out of her skin.

"When he died, he had a wife."

"You mean that little tramp." Red stained her cheeks and her voice rose about an octave.

"Well, since they were legally married, she was his heir to at least half of everything he owned." I drew it out as long as possible. "The Probate Court might come up with answers that you haven't begun to dream of." I turned toward the front door.

The old housekeeper's face changed to a bluish-gray and her chin wobbled. For her to change colors that rapidly, she must have had a chameleon slithering around in her family tree.

"Oh. By the way." I spun around and walked back to her. "Mrs. Gardiner told me she fired the housekeeper. If you've been here for more than twenty years, then you must be the one she fired. Am I right?" I didn't give her a chance to regain her composure.

"Mr. Samuel gave my job back." Her voice shook more than her hands. "He said that nothing she did counted." She responded with a rebellious tilt of her chin.

"Mr. Samuel must be getting his money's worth." I trailed a finger across a dusty table and made a show of looking at the dirt I picked up.

"I'm to stay here, but there's no money for a cleaning staff."

"When I talk to the police about coming here, who may I say I spoke with?" I dug my notebook out of my shoulder bag.

She seemed reluctant to answer so I stepped around her toward the French doors. "Perhaps whoever is listening behind these doors will be able to identify you."

Catching my arm to stop me, she cleared her throat. "I'm Margo Baca."

The muffled slither of footsteps echoed in the musty hall. I tried to cover my interest by rifling through my purse for a pen. I expected a lot of things, yet two Bacas in less than twenty-four hours couldn't be charged to coincidence.

"Do you have any relatives in New Mexico?" I thumbed through my notebook, looking for a clean page.

She glared at me with a sullen expression that made her look as friendly as a rattler with a stomach ache. "Why do you want to know?"

"I research genealogy in my spare time." I knew that truth would be a stranger to any answer she gave. "Do you know anybody named Juan Baca in New Mexico?"

I worked my way slowly around the entry hall. I wanted to see who or what was hiding behind the double doors.

"I've answered all the questions I plan to." She walked toward the front door. "You need to leave."

I was too close to back off now. I reached for the handle of the closest door and shoved it open. Who or what had been listening was gone. It looked like a formal living room. The walls were bare and the few pieces of furniture looked like garage sale leftovers. Either the Gardiners had no taste or someone had stripped everything of value from the room.

Margo Baca recovered in time to grab my arm before I could open any more doors. She hustled me out and slammed the door quicker than a night nurse handing out sleeping pills.

I wondered if the rest of the house had been stripped. I figured the furnishings probably measured up to the rest of the neighborhood at one time. From the large clean patches on the wallpaper, it hadn't been long since the art work had been removed. Scratches in the parquet flooring looked like something heavy had been dragged across it.

Samuel Gardiner had my vote as the family furniture mover and I hadn't even taken a look at his pecs.

****

I cooled my heels until Liam got back from a court appearance. I read everything on his desk and started on the bulletin board when he and Ciardi walked in.

"Whaddo you want?" Ciardi dropped into Liam's desk chair.

"A lot of things." I showed him all my teeth. "But not a single one of them involves your body."

I signaled for Liam to step into the hall. There are times when the thought of staying in the same room with Max Ciardi makes murder seem like too good an idea to pass up.

Liam grabbed his hat and told Ciardi that he'd be back after lunch. We headed north at a fast pace. He never asked me where I wanted to go for lunch. Molly's Café was the only place he thought served a decent lunch and, if I didn't want to eat their food, he just considered it a good way to save money. Liam ordered two specials, coffee for himself and a diet soda for me.

"Well?"

I felt my phone buzz, pulled it out of my pocket and saw the caller ID read *Name Withheld*. I held up a finger. "Excuse me. I need to take this." I stood up and moved away from the table. I punched the answer button. "St. James Investigations."

"I need your help." The caller spoke with a soft, feminine voice.

"How can I help you?"

The sounds of Waylon Jennings and loud laughter almost drowned out her voice. "I have lost something that I really need."

"Finding missing items is not what I normally do." The background noise didn't bode well for this call. "What exactly did you lose? Do you have any idea where to look?"

"The last time I had it was at work this afternoon." The voice changed from soft to distant as if the phone had moved away from her mouth.

"Where have you looked for it?"

"Just everywhere."

"I need to know what you lost before I can commit to helping you."

"Well," she paused then started giggling. "I lost my mind."

"That's obvious." Another drunk entertaining her friends. I turned off the phone and shoved back in my pocket and returned to my seat.

"What's obvious?"

"Someone had too much to drink and decided it would be fun to call a private detective." I reached for a napkin. "Has Caroline Gardiner's will been probated?"

"Ronald Gardiner's original will had been filed in probate court, but she died before the hearing."

"Did she leave a will?" I leaned to one side so the waitress could hit the table with our plates. The first couple of times I went to Molly's with Liam, I ended up with salad in my lap. The waitress had a thing for Liam and thought I might be competition for his affections.

"That's up to the lawyers and judges to sort out. Why?" He poked around in his salad bowl. Liam always did that and it drove me nuts. About the time he got his driver's license, he found a microscopic insect on a piece of lettuce and he's still searching for its mate.

"I went out there this morning."

"You should've told me." He took a huge bite of his salad. "I could've saved you some time. The place is to stay sealed until the court can decide who gets what."

"The court must've made a decision and not informed you." I sniffed at the chunks of tofu in my salad.

"Whatareyoutalkingabout?" he said through a mouthful. He ate like a backhoe, and sometimes it was better to wait until he shoveled it all in before you got down to business.

"I didn't see the house before they died, but my best guess is that somebody stripped it of everything of value."

"I was out there right after Caroline Gardiner's death and helped seal it up." He mumbled through a glob of tofu. "It takes a court order to unseal it."

"Did you explain it to the housekeeper and Ronald's brother?" I pushed my plate away. I couldn't choke down any more of it.

"There was no housekeeper." He began to chew faster and faster. "They fired the last one and we couldn't find the butler."

I gave him a rundown on my visit with Margo Baca and the mysterious moving door. I included a summary evaluation of the housekeeping service and the quality of their work. While I rattled on about the furnishings and landscaping, Liam signaled the waitress for the bill and pulled out his cell phone. He glared at her as if nasty looks would make her move faster.

Ciardi must have answered on the first ring because Liam immediately ordered him to get a department car and meet us outside the restaurant five minutes ago. The trip back to the Gardiner house was so fast that I only had time to exchange a couple of insults with Max.

No one answered the bell. I stayed at the front door while Liam and Ciardi went around the house. I doubted if there was anyone left to come flying out the door, so I poked around the bushes and checked the mailbox. I didn't find anything, but moving around kept me from looking like a deranged cosmetic saleswoman.

When doorknob rattled, I ducked behind a shrub, my gun nestled in my hand, when Ciardi poked his head out.

"A little jumpy today, aren't we?" He spun on his heel and laughed as he disappeared into the hall.

A transient vision of him being pushed off a cliff into the mouth of a huge pink alligator swimming in a river of business cards passed before my eyes. It was all that kept me from firing a shot at his over-rated rump.

Margo Baca, the eavesdropper, and most of the furnishings could not be found. Ciardi called a forensics team and notified the law firm handling the estate. Liam called a cab for me and took down a description of the Baca woman while we waited.

He wanted to know where I was going and I told him that I needed to get to know my client better. He directed me to the old gypsy near Fisherman's Wharf who advertised discounts for daytime séances and palm readings.

Chapter 6

When I needed documents from the California Department of Vital Statistics in Sacramento, Maxine Shields was my best source. Most police employees won't help a PI, but she was married to my last partner before I quit the force. She faxed me copies of Caroline's birth certificate and marriage license.

Her birthplace seemed like the best place to start. After I checked with the DMV to make sure her parents hadn't moved, I booked a flight to the Needles Airport.

My stomach snarled. I tried to convince it that Liam's cereal had been nourishing. Contrary to dieticians everywhere, my system can't survive without at least one greasy meal daily featuring red meat, refined sugar, and bleached flour.

I touched the cabby's shoulder. "Pull in at that drive in." Any semi-respectable teenage hangout could be counted on to fulfill my gustatory cravings.

He signaled a right turn. "Are you sure, lady? This place is about to be shut down again by the health department."

"That's the only recommendation I need." The aroma of old grease made my stomach sit up and beg.

He glanced at me in the mirror. "They closed this place last month after the cook started a hepatitis epidemic. He didn't wash his hands and the owner was too cheap to hire a translator so he could be taught elementary hygiene. It ain't natural to eat anything American cooked by someone from Eastern Europe." Mr. Doom kept right on drilling but he never struck oil.

I ordered a burger with double meat, extra bacon, heavy on the onions and mayonnaise with a side order of cheese fries.

The cab driver popped a handful of antacids. "Lady, why don't you just get a gun and shoot yourself?" He belched and took a swig from a bottle of chalky-looking pink stuff. "Just watching you gives me heartburn." He wiped his mouth with the back of his hand.

This guy ought to get together with Liam. When it comes to my diet, they have a lot in common. While the cabbie preached about nutrition, longevity, and bran-enriched diets, I enjoyed every greasy, life-threatening bite. I wiped the shine off my fingers and handed him the greasy napkin along with his tip. When I hopped out, I saw him staring at the soiled napkin as if it had belonged to Typhoid Mary.

I cleared the check-in desk with ten minutes to spare. I picked up a newspaper and some pork rinds for the flight, then leaned against the wall behind one of those Pay-TV chairs. The newscaster smiled her way through a child molestation, four robberies, two murders, and a cop shooting. Too bad a bus loaded with little old ladies hadn't rolled into the bay—she would've really enjoyed that.

My flight was scheduled for one o'clock that afternoon. I usually end up flying at night when almost everyone falls asleep so I don't have to make small talk with seatmates. No beverage carts blocked the aisle, no loud music leaked out of earphones, no whining children. The biggest challenge was making it to the restroom without crashing into people's body parts hanging out in the aisle.

The unoccupied seat beside me eliminated the possibility of having to chat with a fellow flier. My thoughts were interrupted by the occasional snort of laughter from the man behind me. I reread my notes about the Gardiner murders and scribbled some questions I needed answered. I knew why they were killed. Ronald Gardiner's family wanted their money. But what did Margo and Juan Baca stand to gain? I couldn't figure out why they were even a part of the plot. Caroline said something about food in the attic. Was that the Baca connection? Perhaps there were two-legged rats residing under the eaves. I would have Liam check the attic when I got back.

****

Caroline Rand Gardiner's family lived in the outskirts of Needles. Their small ranch house needed paint and the grass looked as beaten down as the rest of the neighborhood. An irregular baseball diamond was worn between two old trees and the gatepost. Home plate was an old sofa cushion. A couple of plastic chairs sat under a medium-sized blue oak and a straggly pinyon tree grew by the front door.

I rang the doorbell. I couldn't hear it ring, but the sound of laughter and indistinct muttering voices drifted through the door. I knocked and the noise died down. An older woman wearing Bermuda shorts and a Needles Football Mom t-shirt opened the door. She looked like a movie mother. She was a little overweight, her short red hair was touched with gray, and her eyes were framed by wrinkles.

"I'm looking for Caroline Gardiner's family," I said. "According to my research, she grew up at this address."

The woman turned her head as if she were slightly deaf. "I have a daughter named Caroline, but her last name is Rand not Gardiner. Why do you ask?"

I introduced myself and showed her my ID. "I have been hired to look for Caroline's family." I held out her birth certificate. "Is this your daughter?"

She looked at the paper and nodded.

At least I had the right address, but she was a little behind the times. It was possible that I would be the bearer of bad news. "May I come in and speak with you about Caroline?"

She pulled open the door. A man and six kids, ranging from elementary to collage age stared at me. They looked like a hard-working family. From the appearance of the living room, they were clean, tidy, and struggling to making ends meet.

The woman extended her hand. "I'm Emily and that man over there is Harley. We're Caroline's parents."

"It's nice to meet you." I checked their names with those I had found on Caroline's birth certificate.

When a teenage boy rose from a thread-bare easy chair and offered me a place to sit, I noticed that the man next to him was in a wheelchair. He had a piece of tape across his nose and two black eyes. His unbuttoned shirt revealed a large bandage and he had a soft cast on his left leg.

"If you'll excuse me, I need to lie down." As he started rolling toward a hallway, Harley took over and pushed him out of the room.

"That's our son Mike," Emily said.

I shook my head. "He must have had some bad luck." I was nosy enough to want all the details, but trying to be discreet enough not to ask.

"He was doing a first-year medical externship at a hospital when he was attacked by a patient." His mother's voice broke and I saw tears in her eyes.

"Did that happen here?"

"No." She wiped her eyes and cleared her throat. "He was assigned to a hospital north of Redding. A woman stabbed him on his first day there."

"How did she get hold of a knife?" This sounded a lot like how Mandy got out of the hospital. "Do you have any idea who the woman was?"

"No one knew where she got the knife." Emily shook her head. "All Mike remembers was he never saw the woman before she struck out and slashed him across the chest. He broke his nose and injured his leg when he fell trying to get away from her."

"That's terrible." I tried to think of some appropriately sympathetic words. Everything I thought of seemed inadequate. "Did he find out the name of his attacker?"

"No. The authorities wouldn't tell us who stabbed him because she was a patient. They claimed that identifying her would violate her right to privacy. Of course, they were just trying to avoid being sued."

The whole stabbing business made me feel even worse about Caroline's murder. I would have walked out the door and never looked back if I hadn't felt partly responsible for her death.

"You wanted to speak with us about Caroline.

What do you want to know?" asked Emily.

I thumbed through my notebook while I gathered my thoughts. "When was the last time you heard from her?"

Harley came back into the room. "What's this about? Has something happened to our daughter?"

I was not ready to tell them about Caroline's death. I might get more information if I could delay the notification. So I ignored their questions and forged ahead. "When was she here last?"

They hadn't seen or heard from her in about three months.

"Why did she leave?" I asked.

Her parents exchanged worried looks as if they did not know how much to trust me. "Uh." Harley cleared his throat. "She had some difficulty with a man she was dating."

"What kind of trouble?"

"If we explain it, you must be careful who you share it with," said Emily. She clasped her shaking hands in her lap.

I assured them that anything they told me would be held in the strictest confidence.

"Okay," her husband continued. "She was dating a deputy sheriff. One night he got drunk and laughed about his former fiancée's death."

"Caroline knew the girl and that she had died after a brutal rape." Her mother continued. "He showed up drunk later that week for a date and started fighting with her. When he put his hands around her neck and shook her head back and forth, she thought he was going to kill her."

Caroline must have been born under a dark star. It

seemed like her bad luck started long before I met her. "Was that when she left home?" I asked.

"She left the next day to stay with a friend in San Francisco," her father said.

Harley shuffled through a sheaf of papers in the top drawer of a writing desk. He wrote Caroline's friend's name and address on a slip of paper as well as the name of the ex-boyfriend and handed it to me. "That was the last time we saw her. Has something happened to Caroline?"

When I worked for the police department, I had managed to avoid one of the requirements—informing families about the death of a loved one. I couldn't handle the grief of the living then, and now it was worse. I never knew exactly what to say, and now I had to be the bearer of bad news.

I started with a little background. "I met Caroline when she wanted to engage me to look into some problems she was having. I didn't think I could help her and refused the job."

"What problems?" asked one of the teenagers who sat quietly on the floor beside his mother's feet.

If they heard about her problems, they might get a rope and hang me from one of those big trees in the front yard. I was not proud of my response to Caroline's plea. Hindsight has always been really good at pointing out my mistakes. "She thought someone was trying to kill her, but it sounded so improbable, I didn't believe her."

"Why would someone want to kill Caroline?" asked her father.

"Caroline married a wealthy man named Ronald Gardiner. When he died, she started having accidents."

I paused groping for the words that might soften the bad news about their daughter's death. "The police notified me that she had been murdered in a hotel room the night after I met her."

The color leached from Emily's face and her husband looked as if he was carved out of wood. I gave them all of the details I knew.

"I am sorry to be the one to tell you about Caroline's death." I had the suffocating feeling that if I stayed longer, I would need tissues myself. "You need to contact Ronald Gardiner's attorneys. A lawyer named Jesse Duke can help you with all the details and answer your questions." I handed Mrs. Rand a slip of paper with the firm's address and phone number. As an afterthought I added Liam's number.

I left it to the Rands to handle the mess someone made of Caroline's life. Will Rogers once said that Henry Ford didn't leave us how he found us, but it would be years before we would understand how much he changed us. When I left the Rands, I knew what I told them changed their lives, but they had no way of knowing how much.

****

I understood why Caroline's clothes did not match her story, but I now had another name for the suspect pool—Deputy Larry McCall. I stopped by the San Bernardino County Sheriff's office and asked for him.

A receptionist with Wanda embroidered on her shirt pocket said he was no longer working for their office. When I asked to speak with the sheriff, she showed me into his office. The faded paint was mostly hidden by pictures of a tall thin man shaking hands with half the politicians in California. Pictures of governors

Brown and Schwarzenegger shared the space behind the sheriff's chair, making it look like he was in office by divine right. Wanda directed me to a butt-sprung leather chair and said the sheriff would be right in.

The sheriff huffed through the door. "What can I do for you, little lady?" He settled in his chair and pushed his Stetson back with one finger. His big smile showed a lot of tobacco-stained teeth.

I introduced myself and told him I was investigating Caroline Rand's death. I omitted the Gardner as I didn't want to confuse him with her married name. "Can you tell me about a deputy named Larry McCall?"

"Why do you want to know about him?"

"I understand Caroline was dating him before she moved to San Francisco," I said. "Do you know if he has been in contact with her in the last three months?"

The sheriff cleared his throat and rocked back in his chair. He stared at me for a while. "Well." He stretched the word into about five-syllables. "I don't know exactly where he is now. The last I heard he was in custody in Lee County. He beat up a woman in Auburn and I heard he hadn't made bail yet."

"When did that happen?"

"About two or three months ago." He rubbed the stubble on his chin. "I fired him as soon as I heard about his arrest. Wanda can give you the date."

Armed with the date and a phone number for the Lee County sheriff, I took a taxi back to the Needles airport and checked on flights to Auburn. I pulled a book out of my backpack and settled in for a three-hour wait.

Chapter 7

Needles was located on the edge of the Mojave Desert. Even with the Colorado River running through it, cactuses grew better than grass, and the dry, hot wind left me tasting the grit that covered everything.

When I stepped out of the Auburn Airport, it was as if I had landed in another country. The sun, sparkling through the pines and aspens, cast shadows that reminded me of the pictures I had seen of the alpine towns in Austria. With the temperature at least twenty-five degrees cooler than Needles, I turned off the air conditioning in my rental car and enjoyed the cool breeze rushing in through the open windows. I could smell the aroma of cut grass and summer flowers.

The nondescript gray granite building could have passed as half of all the jails in America. The odor of disinfectant mingled with sweat greeted me as I pulled open the front door. A large man sitting behind a tall desk looked up from his newspaper and frowned at me. He was puffing on the stub of a cigar.

"I need to speak with one of your prisoners." I tried not to breathe through my nose. "What do I need to do to see him?"

"See that stack of yellow paper over there?" He pointed with his cigar to a table beside the door. "Fill out one, then give it to me."

It called for the usual *who are you* and *who do you want to see* with a large space for an essay answer about why. I knew the drill so I didn't argue. I gave the completed form to the desk sergeant and asked how long it would be before I could speak with McCall.

He grunted and pushed a button. The door behind him opened and an armed officer signaled me to follow him into another room. Nodding toward a visitor's chair, he stared at the yellow form and then at me.

"How did you find out that McCall was in jail here?"

"His former employer, the sheriff in Needles, told me this was the last place he'd heard McCall was." I pulled out my identification from my bag. "He was dating a woman who was murdered in San Francisco. I have been hired to investigate her death."

"That sounds like something the police should be investigating instead of a P.I." He leaned back and stared at me through half-closed eyes. "Why you?"

"A member of the family paid me to look for answers." I omitted a few details. "The police are also investigating, but with budget cutbacks, they can't afford to run all over the state asking questions."

He stood and adjusted his gun belt. "I'll check to see if he wants to talk to you. Wait here." He said as he went out the door.

One hour and four chapters later, the officer came back. "McCall will talk to you tomorrow. He wants his lawyer with him."

"Okay." I packed the book in my bag. "What time do I need to be back?

"Nine."

****

56

My nine o'clock appointment was rescheduled. McCall or his lawyer had overslept. With luck, both of them would be up and about by two. I killed the time eating lunch at a little outdoor cafe.

When I stepped into the waiting room the ambiance had not improved since yesterday. I am not much of a housekeeper, but I had an urge to dust the furniture and straighten up wanted posters. Some of the notices on the bulletin board had yellowed and begun to crumble from age. The newer ones were stapled randomly over the older notices giving the appearance of a refrigerator covered with kindergarten artwork. The NO SMOKING sign needed to be taped atop the front desk. The officer's cigar smoke made my eyes water.

"Ms. St. James." The lieutenant I spoke with yesterday called from the door to his office. "Mr. McCall's attorney is tied up in court and won't be here for at least another hour."

"Is there any chance the McCall will speak to me without him?"

"Nope." He closed the door before I could ask anything else.

I stepped out onto the cement stoop for fresh air. I felt like swearing or shooting the lieutenant. Neither would solve anything. Make-the-PI-wait was a game I was familiar with since I had to deal with police officers routinely.

I sat on the steps and called Liam. Maybe he had found out something about Caroline's murder.

"Where are you?" he asked.

"I'm in Auburn."

"What are you doing there?"

I explained about finding Caroline's family in

Needles. "They said she left when she found out her boyfriend had beaten up another woman. I'm here trying to see him."

"What's the problem?" Liam asked. I could hear the thump of his feet landing on top of his desk.

"Well, he is in jail here for beating up another woman." I coughed to clear my throat. "He won't see me without his lawyer who might be stuck in court or on a golf course."

"They giving you the run around?"

"Oh yeah. You would think the lieutenant was Ciardi's first cousin. They have a lot in common."

I heard Max snort in the background. Liam had a love affair with his speaker phone. "If I wanted to speak to your demented partner, I would call him."

I heard Liam lift the receiver. "Why did you call?"

"Caroline's family hadn't heard she died. I gave them your information and told them to get in touch with you. I didn't mention the money, but I suspect they'll inherit a bundle. It looked like they need it."

The door swung open behind me. "Ms. St. James," the desk sergeant said in his low, grating voice. "McCall's lawyer is here."

"Talk to you later." I punched the disconnect button.

The cop led me to a small room where the table and chairs were bolted to the tiled floor. The dingy walls were covered with a variety of splotches. I couldn't tell what they were nor did I want to know. A man in a rumpled suit with his collar open and tie hanging loose lounged in one chair looking at the yellow paper I had filled out. The other man wore an orange jumpsuit.

"I am Aggie St. James. I need to ask Mr. McCall some questions."

"You may ask, but I'll decide what he'll answer. His current charges are off the table."

"I'm only interested in what he knows about Caroline Rand." I pulled my notebook out of my bag.

"What about her?" McCall asked. His voice sounded like a growl.

"Have you seen her since she left Needles?"

"Why do you wanna to know?" He asked as he slouched lower in his chair.

"Do you know why she left Needles?" I didn't expect anything that resembled the truth, but it might get me something.

"I don't know. We went out one night and when I called her two days later, she was gone." He sat up straighter. "Is that any way to treat the man you're supposed to marry?"

"You were engaged?" That was news. Her parents hadn't mentioned a pending marriage.

"Yeah. It's a good thing I hadn't given her a ring or I'd be stuck with paying for it."

"You haven't seen her since she left?"

His lawyer leaned in. "He's answered the question. Move on or we leave."

I closed my notebook and sat back. "I suppose you'll find out soon enough. Caroline was murdered last week. Do you know anyone who would want her dead?"

"What happened to her?"

I explained about her death and the circumstances surrounding it.

"Well, it wasn't me. I've been locked up here for

three months." McCall stood up. "I've said all I'm going to."

I remained seated while the two men filed out. That was a waste of time. I hoped he might be willing to talk about why she left home. I still did not know what happened between the time she left home and her marriage to Gardiner.

****

I tried to breathe in the clean mountain air as I left the police station, but the desk sergeant's cigar smoke followed me. A picture of a cartoon character with a boiling cloud of smoke obscuring his vision flitted through my mind. I could still smell the smoke on my clothes as I climbed into my rental car.

My cell phone chirped. The caller ID said "unknown number" and when I answered it, I could hear car noises and a radio playing a country song I couldn't identify.

"St. James Investigations."

The caller made a throat-clearing noise then hung up. I punched the redial and an electronic voice said that the number was no longer working. Again. This was the third hang up this week. It was not unusual to get a few of these calls, but with Liam's ex-wife on the loose, those calls disturbed me.

My flight wasn't scheduled for a couple of hours. While sitting in the Auburn airport, I thumbed through my notes. I needed to find out what happened to Ronald Gardiner's body. Where was it? If I arranged for it to be transported back to San Francisco, could another autopsy with a drug panel be performed? Or was it too late?

The Baca woman and the cop with the same last

name had a half dozen question marks in my notes. Margo Baca knew the answers some of my questions, but I needed for Liam to ask them. She was not forthcoming when I met her at the Gardiner mansion. The policeman in New Mexico had been equally reticent.

With more questions than answers, I settled into my seat, prepared to sleep through the flight. My seatmate apparently had taken an afternoon nap and was ready to chat with anyone with a pulse. I pulled an eye mask from my carryon and pretended to be asleep. She ignored the mask and my silence. She spent the entire flight talking about her grandchildren, the neighbor's chickens, and every trip she had taken since puberty. Her nonstop yakking gave me a headache the size of Wyoming.

When I deplaned in San Francisco, I skipped the luggage return and went out to the line of taxis in front of the terminal. Someone bumped me as I signaled for a cab. At first glance, I thought it was the woman who had been seated in front of me on the plane. When I took a closer look, I realized she was wearing a wig that was slightly askew. The woman walked with a slight limp. Her lingering perfume ticked a cord in my memory. It was a familiar scent, but the snare drum in my head kept me from recognizing it. Maybe I would remember where I had smelled it after a handful of aspirin and an overdue nap.

****

"I'm getting hang ups complete with odd noises and breathing," I said. "When I tried redialing, the numbers wouldn't go through."

I had met Liam at Fisherman's Wharf for dinner.

61

He didn't like eating standing up, so I shooed the sea gulls away from the only empty table near my favorite seafood stall. I brushed away the feathers and other unidentifiable debris. Liam took a seat, but he refused to set his plate on the table.

"Anything else?" He dug through his crab salad looking for vermin.

"A woman bumped into me at the airport." I sprinkled vinegar on my fish and chips.

"And?"

"It took a while, but I remembered where I smelled her perfume. It was that awful patchouli oil Mandy wore. You know the one that was used as an insect repellant until the hippies found out it would mask the smell of marijuana. She called it her signature scent, but I'd bet her nose didn't work right."

Liam gave me a pained look over his salad. "That doesn't mean a lot. It's sold everywhere."

"She had a limp and her wig looked like it was about to fall off."

Liam quit digging in his food and stared over the railing at the incoming tide. The setting sun sparkled on the rippling waves. A pair of harbor seals barked at each other under the wharf. Shrieking seagulls danced above the water, diving for bits of food. "I had hoped she'd be picked up before she got this far."

"Does she still have a key to your condo?"

"I had the lock changed after her last visit," he said. His hand trembled as he picked up his cup. Coffee sloshed onto his shirt. "Crap." Slamming the cup down, he reached for a napkin and scrubbed at the spots.

The last time Mandy broke in, she slashed Liam's chest and stabbed him in the leg. He was able to grab her arm and subdue her before she could kill him. He almost bled to death. The doctors at Ashworth hospital assured him that she would never be able to escape their facility again. Apparently, they were wrong.

"What are you going to do?" I asked.

"Max wants me to stay in his apartment." He dropped his salad in the trash. "I don't think it'll help. She knows where he lives. Besides, I don't want to leave Hobo alone."

"Really?"

"The last thing she said as the police took her away was that she would kill him if she ever saw him again. Hobo came to my defense and ripped four bloody stripes down her arm."

Mandy was born beautiful. She spent hours every day maintaining her looks. She believed the accident had disfigured her for life. Even though the reconstructive surgery restored her face and body, when she looked in a mirror, she still saw the scars. The lacerations on her head caused her hair to grow back in patches. She thought that no wig could ever look as good her natural blonde hair.

The accident affected her mind. Liam had told her that the brakes on the MG needed work, but she didn't believe him and refused to drive his pickup truck. Although a California highway patrolman clocked her at eighty on the coast highway just before the crash, Mandy blamed Liam for her injuries. After the surgeries, her behavior became even more irrational and, finally, she had to be hospitalized.

"You need to be careful," he said. "She thinks we were in cahoots when she had the accident."

Chapter 8

Harvey, the office building superintendent, greeted me at the door. "Welcome back, Ms. St. James." Something must have happened. The last time he cornered me at the door a pipe had broken and flooded my office.

"It's good to see you, Harvey." I paused to let him continue. Nothing would speed him up. I caught myself leaning toward him, waiting.

He cleared his throat, rubbed his hands together, and shrugged his shoulders. Every conversation had to wait for him to run through his rituals. Perhaps I frightened him and he needed the protection of his superstitions or he required time to sort out his thoughts. Over the years I had learned he moved on his own schedule. In the mornings, he stationed himself at the elevator, stopping people to chat. He called it socializing with the tenants. Snooping was better word. I ducked out on those daily conversations by taking the stairs in the mornings, but this time I couldn't avoid him.

"Your door has been damaged." He cleared his throat for emphasis. "Of course, we'll add the repairs to your rent."

"What happened?" I asked.

"Someone broke that little window in the door

and...uhm...and tried to reach the door knob." He was rubbing his hands so vigorously I thought of Lady Macbeth.

"And." I tried to encourage him to continue.

"Uh, there was blood on the broken glass and some words painted on the door."

"What did it say?"

He grimaced. "I don't use those words."

"Did you report it to the police?"

"No." He picked a tiny speck of lint from the arm of his ancient woolen sweater. "I didn't see who broke the window and, since the door was still locked, I thought I would just leave that up to you."

"Thanks." I rolled my eyes.

"You're welcome." A big smile lit his face as he turned toward his office.

Sarcasm was lost on him.

When I stepped out of the elevator, I could see the small broken window in my door. When I first moved into the office, I had the glass replaced with a one-way mirror so I could see if I wanted to let the visitor in. A bright red *Die Bitch* was painted across the door. It looked like a child's printing with paint dripping like blood from each letter. No one had covered the broken window and the door was still locked.

I called Liam and asked him if he could come over.

"What's going on?" He was in his car with the window down. I could hardly hear him over the roar of the wind.

I explained about the damage and he told me to wait until he got there. "Don't go in alone." I heard him flip on the siren before he shut off the phone.

****

Liam entered first and pointed to the broken glass on the floor. I stepped over it and scanned the office. Nothing seemed to be missing. It looked like the remaining red paint had been thrown all over the room. The empty can lay in front of my desk with a paintbrush stuck to the desk lamp.

"We might be able to get fingerprints from the brush handle, but I think we both know who they belong to," said Liam. He punched a number into his phone and asked for a crime scene tech to meet us at my office. He pointed to the broken window. "It looks like your burglar's arm was just long enough to reach the door lock."

I peered at the fragments of glass in the door and pointed to some reddish-brown stains. "Yes. It looks like she was bleeding when she turned the doorknob. I don't think she could've splashed this much paint around simply by throwing it through the window"

"We'll have the tech sample that blood, too. I'm pretty sure it's Mandy's."

I stared at the paint spatters on the desk, file cabinet, and floor. The damage was minor, but housework wasn't my thing and this cleanup would require a lot of elbow grease. I touched a dry red spot. Add paint thinner and a scraper to the job.

Liam looked around the office, a puzzled frown on his face. "Why do you suppose she took your safe?" He wandered over to where it had set.

"She didn't." I had left the bottom desk drawer open the last time I was there. I pulled out a stack of red-spattered files. "I took it to my apartment a couple weeks ago."

"Why?"

"This building was sold. The new owner thinks he can double his money by upping the rents so the tenants will move out. He plans to convert these offices into condos." I stacked the loose papers from the other drawers atop the files. "My lease is up for renewal. If I want to stay, I'll have to pay an extra five hundred a month."

"That is quite a bump."

"Basically, I just store notes and files here." I picked up the petty cash that had been strewn around. "I seldom have a client come in, so I'm going to work out of my apartment for a while."

"Good luck with that."

"Do you suppose she continued her art work at my apartment?" I looked at the epithet on the door. The first time Mandy had escaped, she painted an extended message on the wall that ran from husband-stealing whore to comments about my ancestors. That cleanup only required a coat of paint.

"I gave Ciardi my key and sent him over there, but he hasn't called back." Liam looked at his watch. "I should've heard from him by now." He tapped a number into his phone and listened for a few seconds. "Something's wrong. Max always answers by the third ring. Let's go."

****

The late afternoon traffic inched along as the watery sunlight broke through the heavy rainclouds. Liam honked and swore his way toward my apartment. We went through the intersections with lights flashing. The siren was punctuated by him honking the horn. A couple of pedestrians leapt out of the way and, when I looked back, they were giving us the finger.

"You might want to slow down," I said as we swerved around the corner onto Thirty-Fifth Street. "There's a school on the next block."

Liam growled but he hit the brakes as we entered the school zone. There were no children about, but several parents clogged the street waiting for the dismissal bell. A Jeep Cherokee pulled out in front of us. Liam slammed on the brakes, lay on the horn, and made so much noise the driver ran up onto the curb.

"Goddamn deaf women!" Liam steered around the rear of the Jeep and ran another stop sign.

"That was a man." I braced my hand on the dashboard. "Women know better than to get in your way."

"Smart-ass."

The car screeched to a halt in the loading zone in front of my apartment house. He threw his police sign on the dash while I hurried to jab my code into the outer door lock. We raced up the stairs. My apartment was one of four on the third floor. The door was ajar and red paint was smeared on the door handle and dribbled on the floor.

"Wait," Liam said quietly, his gun in his hand. He signaled for me to step aside.

He pushed the door open. "Come out of there," he shouted. "I've got a gun and I won't hesitate to shoot you."

No one answered. Liam stepped into the living room, looking around. He signaled for me to follow. My computer was overturned, the screen broken. Papers were scattered on the floor. Vases, pictures, and the television were all smashed. The intruder had smeared red paint on just about everything in the room.

I moved to the bedroom. From the door I could see red smeared on the bed and floor. I heard a slight noise. I pulled my Smith and Wesson and motioned for Liam to join me. I leaned in and saw a bloody hand on the floor partially covered with my bedspread. He pointed his gun at it and eased around the end of the bed.

"Oh, God!" He dropped to his knees and laid his gun on the floor. "Call 911."

I holstered my gun and punched the numbers into my phone. I walked over to see what had happened. A bloody body lay on the floor, the large gash from the shoulder across his stomach exposed part of his small intestines. His nose was pushed to the side with a thready stream of blood running down his face.

"Ciardi?" He was so beaten up I hardly recognized him.

"He's still breathing." He threw the bedspread out of the way. "Max? Max? Can you hear me?" Liam's hand shook as he swiped the blood off his face.

Ciardi opened his eyes and moved his lips. Nothing came out.

"Take it easy," Liam said. "Help is on the way."

"I'll go down and make sure the paramedics can get in."

"Go." Liam looked up at me. A single tear slid down his cheek. "I'll take care of Max."

I went down in the elevator and turned it off so it would be there for the paramedics. The ambulance pulled up just as I opened the outer door. I told the EMTs where to go then followed them into the elevator. They asked about the victim and I told them what I knew.

My best guess was that Mandy had attacked him.

She hadn't liked Max any more than me. She believed we had broken up her marriage and turned Liam against her.

Usually paramedics check vital signs, start IVs, and bandage bleeding limbs. This time they did a grab-and-go so they could get Ciardi to the hospital as soon as possible. I had only seen this maneuver once when the victim was so seriously injured that death was imminent. The paramedics called it running hot, all lights blazing and making enough noise to scare the deaf. Max was breathing when they took him, but he had lost so much blood that he would be taken straight into the operating room.

Liam tossed his car keys to me and climbed into the back of the ambulance. I watched it scream down the street until it was out sight.

The building custodian was already mopping blood off the elevator floor. He paused long enough to point toward the stairs with his chin. I ran back up to my apartment. A patrolman had already stretched crime scene tape across the hall on both sides of my door.

"I need to get a few things out of there." I bent to go under the tape.

He moved in front of me. "You'll wait until the crime scene people get finished."

I held out my ID. "I live here."

"You still have to wait."

Arguing wouldn't help. When one policeman has been attacked, the others closed ranks and it wouldn't matter what you wanted. I stepped back and punched Liam's number into my phone. I heard a busy signal. He was probably calling Ciardi's family. I slid down the wall and sat, waiting for the crime scene techs.

Depending on the number of crimes today, it might take them a long time to get here.

The furniture came with the apartment and I could buy more clothes. The small cedar box in the back of the closet was the most valuable thing I owned. It held the detritus of my marriage: the flag that had been draped over my husband's coffin, his badge, and class ring. The crumbling corsage I had worn to our wedding lay on top of the little notes he left for me while I slept and he went to work. Our wedding rings rattled around loose in the bottom of the box.

I have tried to stay busy so I couldn't dwell on the pieces of a life that I lost far too soon. But the memories marched like a military parade through my mind while I waited outside the door.

Another cop I didn't recognize came to relieve the first one.

"Have you heard any news from the hospital?" I asked.

He shook his head as he took his place in front of the open door. "He was in surgery the last I heard."

"Any chance I can go in and get something from the closet?"

"No." He sounded like a pissed off grizzly.

I took out my notebook and thumbed through the pages, trying to piece together Caroline Gardiner's life. Perhaps I would do a better job with hers than I had with my own.

****

The crime scene investigators turned up more than an hour after Ciardi had been hauled out of my apartment. I recognized Kathy Garber from the time I spent on the force. She and I had investigated several crimes together before she worked the scene where my husband had been shot. I described the small wooden box that I wanted from my closet. She said she would bring it to me if it wasn't a part of the scene.

I tried to reach Liam while I waited for Kathy to return. His phone was still busy. I gave up when she came out with my box.

"I can't give it to you," she said. "It looks like someone tried to pry it open with a bloody knife. It's still locked."

"Thanks," I said, relieved. "Please make sure it doesn't disappear. It's the only thing I want from the apartment."

Reassured, I left for the hospital. Liam would be there as long as Ciardi was in surgery. They had been partners for years and their bond ran deep. I was not sure how Liam could stand Max for that long and, when I asked him about it, he said it was a man thing that I wouldn't understand.

The hall leading to the waiting room was lined with police officers, some in uniform, others in street clothes. I recognized a few of them from my time on the force. Manny Shields, my old partner, directed me toward the surgery waiting room. I found Liam staring out the window at the Bay Bridge. I stood beside him until he spoke.

"Max is still in surgery." His voice reflected his tension. "At the last update, he was still on a respirator and receiving blood as fast as they could pump it in."

"Do they think he'll make it?"

"The doctor said he has a chance if they can control the infection from the stomach wound."

"Have they caught up with Mandy yet?"

"No." He spoke through clenched teeth. "The last sighting was at the bus station. Someone saw her in the restroom washing blood off her arms and legs. By the time the officers got there, she'd disappeared."

Max's mother and sister Angela sat huddled together, speaking quietly in Italian. Mrs. Ciardi had immigrated after she married an American sailor she met in Genoa. She still had difficulty understanding English and she needed Angela to translate for her. She would point at Liam and he would shake his head. Her sniffles spoke a universal language.

"You need to go home," he said after an hour. "Crime scene should be finished."

"I'll stay. Kathy Garber will lock up," I said. "She knows what I want out of there."

A doctor came into the waiting room and asked for the Ciardi family. Liam introduced him to Max's mother and sister and asked how Max was doing.

"He's in recovery." He stretched and rubbed the back of his neck. "We have done everything we can. Now we wait. It'll take time for him to heal." He paused long enough for Angela to translate, then he added, "One of the nurses will come and take his family back."

"How badly was he hurt?" Liam asked before the doctor could leave.

"He has three stab wounds. The one across his abdomen is the worst and he needed several units of blood. We'll keep him on the respirator until he regains consciousness and then we'll see if he can breathe on his own."

The nurse came in and beckoned the Ciardis to follow. Liam went out to talk to the waiting officers while I settled in with the last cup from the urn.

The smell of disinfectant laced with the burnt smell of the coffee reminded me of all the times I had spent in waiting rooms. Quiet footsteps hustled past the door tending to the business of helping the sick and injured.

My husband died after three days in a critical care ward here. It was a long time before I could even walk into this waiting room let alone visit someone here. It wasn't until Mandy stabbed Liam that I came back again.

I would wait with Liam just he had stayed with me all those years ago.

Chapter 9

Liam stared out the dark window toward the lights on the bay bridge. "What are you charging now?"

"Huh?" I looked up from the article about salmon fishing in *National Geographic*. The magazine cover was missing and the first dozen pages were so tattered as to be unreadable.

"How much does it cost to hire your services?"

"It depends on the client's ability to pay. Why do you want to know?"

He rubbed his forehead and pulled on his left ear, all signs he was clearly agitated. "I want to hire you to stay with Max."

"Won't he have a deputy stationed outside the room?"

"Yes, but I want someone with him. The deputies assigned to this kind of job will never be nominated for officer of the year." Liam sat down beside me.

"Screwups?" I put the magazine back on the table.

"Probably. The force is short-handed and no one can be spared to stay with him. I want someone I can trust in the room when I can't be there."

"Do you think Mandy will try again?"

Liam's ex-wife was insane. The doctor who treated her said she probably showed symptoms before the car wreck, but no one recognized them. Although she was beautiful and well-educated, she was insecure and needed constant praise. The wreck intensified her neurosis into psychotic behavior. She blamed Liam, Max, and me for her injuries. Every time she looked in a mirror, she saw ghosts of the scars that had been surgically removed and her rage built. When Liam encouraged her to see a psychologist, she had refused.

"I don't want to take a chance until she is locked up or dead." Liam turned to stare out the window again.

Mandy had destroyed any feelings Liam had for her when she stabbed him.

As she attacked him, Hobo had lashed at her, scratching her hand and arm. She swung the knife at the cat and chopped off the last three inches of his tail. Damage to the cat bothered Liam more than his own stab wounds.

"Do you want me to take the day or night shift?" I wasn't getting anywhere on Caroline Gardiner's case, so putting it aside for a few days would not matter.

"I'm on the night shift this month," he said. "If you can take the nights, I'll be here during the days. Stay in my apartment until you find somewhere to live. Your place is a mess."

****

I relieved Liam in time for him to make his eleven o'clock shift. The deputy guarding the door was leaned back in the chair with his chin resting on his chest. He was supposed to check everyone's ID before they entered Ciardi's room, but he didn't even look up when I walked in the door.

"I see why you want someone in here with Max." I nodded toward the sleeping deputy.

"I'll wake him up before I leave."

"Have there been any changes?" I settled in the chair Liam vacated and placed my revolver on the table next to the telephone.

"The doctor thinks Max might be unconscious for another day or two." Liam pulled on his jacket. "You might want to cover that gun. If a nurse sees it and screams, it might wake the deputy."

I heard the deputy snort when Liam kicked his chair on the way out. He looked around to see who had disturbed him. He peered into the room and saw me sitting beside the bed.

"Who are you?"

"If you had been doing your job when I came in, you wouldn't have to ask."

He stepped into the room and glared at me. "Now listen here, little lady. I asked you a question."

I set my book aside and stood up. I was at least six inches taller than the deputy. He took a quick step back and put his hand on his gun. I learned a long time ago that it was hard to take a man seriously when I towered him. It's even harder to be humble.

"What do you think you are going to do with that gun?"

"I asked for your identification." He stiffened his back and puffed out his chest. He looked like demented blowfish. "If you don't cooperate, I'm going to lock you up."

"On what charge?" I started to ask how he was going to get me to the jail, but thought the better of it.

"Interfering with an officer of the law." He unsnapped his holster and loosened the gun.

Just then the doctor came through the door reading a chart and bumped into the deputy.

"Excuse me." He peered down his nose at him. "Aren't you supposed to be guarding the door?"

He pointed at me. "I was 'til she slipped in and refused to identify herself."

"I'm Dr. Carlton." He extended his hand. "We met the day Detective Ciardi was brought in."

"Aggie St. James."

"The other police officer said you would be here during the night." He eyed the handle of the gun on the table. "He said you're a private detective."

I slid the napkin back over the weapon. "Yes, I am. Liam wanted me here because I can identify the woman who stabbed Max."

"Does he really think she'll show up here with a guard outside the door?" The doctor paused and waited until the deputy looked at him then nodded toward the hall. He waited long enough for the deputy to take his seat before closing the door.

"Mandy is insane. I hope they catch her before she finds out where Max is."

I watched the doctor examine Max's wounds and check his vitals. "How's he doing today?"

"His fever is down and his blood pressure is stable." He scribbled something in the chart. "He should wake up soon. Do I need to request a hospital security guard for the door?"

"It wouldn't hurt. Maybe between two, one of them might stay awake most of the time."

After the doctor left, I checked the hall and closed the door. Mandy might wear a disguise, but her perfume would give her away. The last time I flew in, I bumped into a woman wearing the same perfume. I now believed she could have been Mandy.

Sitting in the hospital room was like watching moss grow on a tree. I turned the light on in the restroom and left the door ajar. There was enough ambient light to see Max's chest rising and falling in time with the wheezing respirator. The only other sounds were the beep of the heart monitor and the buzz of the deputy's snoring. When I checked the hall, the security guard's chair was empty.

I kicked the deputy's chair until he jerked upright, blinking in the bright lights.

"What do ya want?" asked the deputy.

"Sorry to interrupt your nap." I looked toward the nurses' station. "Where is the hospital guard?"

"He's on his dinner break." He leaned his chair back against the wall. "I wasn't sleeping."

"Have you seen anyone who doesn't belong here?"

"No, and I'll thank you to leave me alone so I can do my job."

I scanned the hall. "Try not to snore so loudly that you wake the other patients."

I closed the door and propped a chair under the handle. The early morning hours were the most conducive to sleep. Walking back and forth followed by yoga and calisthenics got me past my usual bedtime. Fear helped. As long as Mandy was free, I knew she would be coming for us.

The door bumped against the chair. I grabbed my gun, leveling it toward the door. "Who's there?"

"Night nurse."

"One moment," I said from behind the door. I moved the chair and indicated for her to come in.

She reached in and flipped the light switch. Keeping her hands turned up, she said, "No weapons."

I put the gun back on the table. "Sorry," I said.

"The charge nurse told me about you." She laid a chart on the bed. "I need to check on the officer."

I watched as she inspected the tubes and listened to Max's chest. She lifted the bandages on his stomach and wrote in his chart.

"How is he doing?"

"Since you aren't a family member, you'll need to talk to the doctor or the family if you want details."

The vigil continued until the early morning light through the eleventh-floor window chased away the dark thoughts I had spent the night with. I was haunted by echoes of the people I had lost: my husband, Liam's mother, and father. Usually, if I could stay busy enough, I could escape the memories in the daylight. Yet, there were times like when I found my apartment trashed, the past could not be ignored.

Liam came to relieve me at eight o'clock. I moved the chair and he came in carrying two cups. He wore the same clothes he had on the night before and he needed a shave.

"Have they found Mandy yet?" I tasted the scalding hot coffee.

"No." He set his cup on the small table beside Max's bed. "How is he doing?"

"I don't know. The nurse wouldn't tell me anything because I'm not a relative."

"You should have claimed to be his wife."

I gathered up my notebook and slipped into my jacket. "Max would shoot me if I tried that."

"Not when he's unconscious."

"But he'll wake up some time." I holstered my gun and picked up my coffee. "I don't want him to come after me for lying to the staff."

I closed the door behind me and noticed that a new deputy was dozing in the hall. I hooked my foot under the chair leg and pulled it away from the wall far enough to make him jump.

"What?" He scrambled up from the chair.

"I wanted to let you know I'm leaving now." Looking back at him as I walked toward the elevators. "There's a strange man in the officer's room. Did you check his identity?"

Guarding an unconscious man was not exciting and I thought the deputy should meet Liam. Finding a police captain in the room might help him stay awake.

When I stepped into the parking lot, I found Manny Shields leaning against my car. He was the last partner I worked with on the force. We had kept in touch over the years. He and his wife always invited me over for holidays. They thought I should not be alone and they were probably right. I could handle all them alone except Christmas. It was the anniversary of the day I got married. Manny kept a bottle of bourbon on hand and, if he poured enough down me to stop the tears, I could make it through the day. The hangover got more spectacular every year.

"What're you doing here?"

"Liam wants me to see that you get to his apartment safely." He held the door for me. "I'll follow you over there. Don't even think about trying to ditch me."

"I'm too tired to argue."

I paused at the exit and waited for Manny to catch up. Together we drove to Liam's condo in parade formation.

Manny stood back until I unlocked the door and shut off the alarm. He walked through the rooms then declared them safe. He remained outside the door until he heard the locks click.

Hobo wrapped around my ankles, meowing loudly. I filled his bowl with crunchies and gave him fresh water.

"You're on your own today." I scratched him behind his ears and gave his tail a tug.

I closed the drapes to shut out the midday sun before I showered and collapsed on Liam's bed. The cat hopped up and curled up next to me as I fell asleep.

****

Hobo growled in my ear. I ignored him until he started licking my eye lids. I swatted at him, but he just growled louder. I peered at my phone. Three o'clock.

"Go back to sleep, cat." I pulled the covers over my head, then he started biting my toes.

I sat up and took a swing at him. Hobo danced out of the way and kept growling, the hair on his tail bristled like a bottle brush. He was focused on the front door. I heard scraping followed by the rattle of the door knob; sounds too soft to wake me.

Clicking off the safety, my revolver pointed at the door, I crept into the living room and took a quick look through the peephole. You can look into a house through a peephole as easily as you can see out them. I should have been able to see the buildings across the street. All I saw was darkness. I grabbed Hobo and stepped away from the door.

"Who's out there?" I shouted.

Shots shattered the air. The cat screeched once and raced under the bed. I flattened myself against the wall.

Six bullets penetrated the metal-covered door followed by the sounds of someone trying to kick it open. I heard a woman's angry voice, but I could not understand the words.

I eased along the wall, through the dead foliage, until I reached my phone. I called 911 and reported the shooting and that someone was trying to break in. Then I punched in Liam's number.

"Someone's trying to get in." My hands were shaking so much I could hardly hold the phone. "Whoever it is shot up your door and tried to kick it open."

"Have you called it in?"

"Yes." I felt my heart slow down and I could breathe easier.

Hobo crept up to me, his hackles up. I sat on the side of the bed and he hopped onto my lap. He was looking for reassurance and I needed a good cuddle. We were still comforting each other when Liam came through the door.

"You all right?" he called, his gun in hand.

"Yes. We're okay." I was relieved to have help.

Liam turned on the lights and looked through the condo. "We? Who's in here with you?"

Hobo leapt toward him and rubbed against his legs. Liam reached down and scratched the cat. "What's with all the purring? You only make that much noise when you've attacked Max."

"We've just spent fifteen minutes in stark terror." I paused long enough to pull on Liam's robe. "Hobo's the hero. He woke me up when someone tried to open the door."

One of the policemen came in carrying a red paint

can. "The wall and door have been smeared with this."

Liam and I stepped out and looked at the door. The words *DIE BASTARD* were smeared across the door and onto the bricks with blobs of red on the step. Scratches ringed the lock. When I saw where a bullet had ripped through the peephole, I started shaking again.

Mandy. She wasn't going to stop until we were either dead or the police could lock her up. The psychosis seemed to be accelerating. She was only a danger to Liam when she was first institutionalized. Now even Max, I, and Hobo were also targets. We understood how the car accident and her insecurities were the roots of her insanity, but it would take a degree in psychology to understand her obsession with red paint.

Liam hosed down the door and wall as soon as the crime scene crew finished taking pictures. Most of the water-based paint came off the door, but the bricks would need sandblasting.

Crime scene tagged and collected the bullets. They used a laser pointer to show the trajectory of each. The shooter had sprayed bullets over the front of the part of the condo. Only the bedroom and kitchen were untouched.

When the techs packed up and left, Liam surveyed the damage. Most of the bullets hit only one wall. One penetrated the picture of Liam on his Officer of the Year plaque. Another shattered a picture of us with his mother. He picked up the picture, carefully removed the glass shards. His muttered curses echoed my feelings. He replaced it on the wall, straightening the frame before getting a broom to clean up the broken glass.

He pulled a bottle of bourbon from the cabinet and splashed some in two glasses. "I'll have a repairman replace the door tomorrow." He pushed one of the glasses toward me. "Drink up."

"Do you think she'll try again?" I watched as he downed the bourbon in one swallow.

"She will, but it's impossible to guess where she'll strike next."

"I could take Hobo to a hotel and he'll be safe."

Liam poured another shot and reached down to run his hand over Hobo's back. He looked like he was running all the alternatives through his mind. He rubbed his thumb and forefinger together, looking at nothing. I knew he would keep that up until he resolved whatever problem was bothering him.

"No." He swirled the bourbon in his glass, then threw it back. "It's better if you two stay here. A unit will be stationed outside. That should keep her from trying again."

"Can she get through the windows that overlook the alley?" I sipped the bourbon. I don't drink often, but a visit from Mandy was a good reason to start.

"I had burglar bars installed after her last visit." Liam looked at the bottle as if he was trying to decide if he needed another shot. "I think you and Hobo will be as safe here as anywhere. Besides he might object to traveling."

Hobo had only left the apartment once since I found him in the rain. It took both of us to wrestle him into a carrier so he could be neutered. The screeching, scratching, and blood-letting was enough for me to swear I would never attempt that again. When Mandy slashed his tail, I called a mobile vet to take care of

85

him. Liam had wanted me to take Hobo to a vet's office, but I paid the extra charges and didn't mention it to him.

"Okay. I'm going back to bed and try to sleep this off," I said moving toward the bed. "Do you still want me to stay with Max tonight?"

Liam just nodded as he left.

Chapter 10

My office was a wreck. I spent half an hour picking my way through the chaos deciding what could be saved. A large rolling trash bin filled with most of the paint- smeared files and books sat outside the door. The ones I needed to save were stacked on the window ledge.

The desk chair looked like someone had been stabbed to death in it. I pushed it into the hall beside the trash can. My desk might be salvageable with some paint thinner and elbow grease. Most of the paint was on the front instead of the working surface. Perhaps I could bequeath the remaining furniture to the next tenant. Let them clean off the paint.

Moving most of my records to my apartment had not saved them from Mandy's wrath. The one good thing about all of that paint was that it forced me to clean out, sort, and dispose of lots of useless paper.

The building manager dropped by to tell me that I would need to vacate until they could repaint the walls and install new carpet. He said it would be several days before I could use it again. Probably I ought to let him know I was not going to renew my lease. But since he was doubling the rent, he should not be surprised.

I took what I could carry to the car. I would have to work like the *Lincoln Lawyer* and do business out of my backseat. The only case that needed my attention was the murder of Caroline Rand Gardener. The police had little to go on and I was stymied by the now-empty mansion and conflicting stories from everyone I had spoken with.

When all else fails, talk to the lawyer. I called the number of the offices of Duke, Smith and Holmes that Caroline had written on her note.

"How may I help you?"

"I need to speak with Jesse Duke."

"Are you a client of his?"

I know receptionists are a necessary fixture in offices, but I consider them a nuisance standing or sitting in my way. "I need to speak with him concerning one of his clients." I identified myself and quit talking. After a long silence, she put me through.

"Jesse Duke." A man with a whiskey tenor answered the phone.

"Mr. Duke. I'm a private investigator hired by Caroline Gardiner. I'd like to speak with you about her death."

He cleared his throat and hesitated. "When did she hire you?"

"I met with her the afternoon before she was murdered. She left a message along with a sum of money asking me to find her killer."

I heard the sound of pages turning then he told someone to cancel an appointment. "I can see you tomorrow afternoon at two. Will that be convenient?"

"I'll be there."

Perhaps the lawyer would have something to say that would help me find out what happened to Caroline. If he wanted to see a copy of the note she left, he would have to wait until I could crack my safe.

****

The deputy was wide awake when I got to Max's room. I showed him my ID and asked if anything unusual had happened. He shook his head and opened the door.

Liam was reading a *Guns and Ammo* magazine with his feet propped on the foot of the bed. The tube had been removed from Max's throat and he looked like he was just sleeping. A bag of clear solution trickled into his arm while amber liquid dribbled into a bag from a tube originating somewhere in his nether regions.

"Has he woken up yet?" I asked.

"No." Liam closed the magazine and handed it to me. "The doctor said he should be waking up any time."

I took Liam's place, tucking my gun under the edge of the mattress. "Have they found Mandy?"

"No," he said as he pulled his coat on. "Every time there's a sighting, she disappears before the cops get there."

"What did you do to the deputy out there? He was actually awake."

"I had a friendly little chat with the sheriff," he said with his hand on the door. "If this one dozes off, he's going to wish they would allow him to guard city dump."

"That's harsh," I said. "What about the hospital security guard? He was snoring the loudest."

"He's the hospital's problem." Liam hesitated and turned back to me. "By the way, the doctor wants someone to talk to him. He thinks Max will wake up sooner if he hears a voice."

"Are you kidding? I had nothing to say to him when he was conscious and nothing comes to mind now."

"Read the magazine to him. He won't know the difference." Liam pulled the door closed.

I shook the magazine at Max. "You'd better appreciate this and wake up before my voice gives out." I looked through the magazine, picked an article about what you need in your camping survival kit for a shelter-in-place scenario.

At two in the morning a nurse wearing a surgical mask and face shield bustled in, straightened the top sheet, and fluffed Max's pillow. She hung a new IV bag and started to leave.

"How is Max doing?" I asked her before she could get to the door.

"Are you a relative?"

"Yes," I lied. I hope Max didn't find out or he might blow a gasket. "I'm his sister."

She peered at me in the dim light. "You don't look much like him."

"Adoption."

"Well," she said. "We won't be able to assess any injuries until he wakes up."

"His...uh...our mother asked me to find out how he is doing today. Is he running a fever or developing an infection?"

The nurse hesitated. Her hand trembled as she reached for the door. "I'm only supposed to start his new IV. You just keep reading to him," she said as she left.

"Well, Max. How would you like to hear an article

about Barrett MRAD sniper rifles used by the Army and Marines?"

I was well into the article when I heard a moan. I looked at Max, but he just lay there with his eyes closed. I found my place and continued the spell-binding piece about sniper rifles.

"Water."

I stood and looked at Max. "Did you say something?"

He cleared his throat then opened one eye and focused on me. "Water." His scratchy voice was hard to understand.

I rang for the nurse. While I waited, I went into the bathroom looking for a glass. There wasn't even a paper cup in the holder.

Five minutes later I considered pulling the alarm cord in the bathroom to get the nurses' attention. Instead, I stepped into the hall and asked the deputy if he had seen a nurse around.

The deputy shook his head. "The only one I saw was the nurse named St. James who went in about twenty minutes ago."

"St. James?" I asked. "Are you sure that was her name?"

"She showed me her name tag and I checked the list of approved visitors. Her name is right here." He pointed to my name on the list.

"Go find a nurse right now." I reached for my cell phone. "What are you waiting for?"

He stood with his chin up and his hand on his revolver. "I'm not to leave the patient unguarded or I'll lose my job."

"Move it, you nitwit. *I'm Aggie St. James*,"

"You're not my boss and I'm not leaving this door no matter what you say," said the deputy. "You go."

"I need to check Max first." I snapped on the overhead lights.

I focused on the IV bag. It looked slightly orange. The last one had been clear. I tried to shut it off, but the clip was missing so I jerked the needle out of his arm. Max watched me with one eye.

"What's going on?" His voice sounded like he had swallowed sandpaper.

"I don't know." I stepped to the door and signaled for the deputy to stand in front of the door.

The deputy closed the door and unsnapped his holster. With his hand on his gun, he edged me farther down the hall.

"I'll go, but don't let anyone else in there until I get back." He flinched at the sound of my cop voice.

I had not used that command tone since I retired from the force. I paused momentarily to appreciate the effect it had on the deputy. He stood a little straighter and sweat beaded on his upper lip. I punched Liam's number in my cell as I sprinted down the hall.

No one was in the nurse's station. I rounded the desk and almost tripped over an upturned chair. Files and papers were strewn across the floor and Max's records were up on the computer monitor.

"You need to get some people over here right now," I said as soon as I heard Liam's voice.

"What's wrong?"

"I'm not sure." I opened a door behind the nurse's desk and found nothing but office and patient supplies. "Someone disguised as a nurse went into Max's room and fiddled with his IV. The real nurse isn't here and whoever was in the nurse's station has been checking Max's records."

"On my way!" he shouted.

I looked in the waiting room then crossed the hall and pushed open the women's restroom door. "Is anyone in here?"

Not receiving an answer, I pushed into the men's room. A pair of legs stuck out from the single stall. A woman in a nurse's uniform lay with her hands and ankles bound together. A handful of paper towels were stuffed in her mouth held in place with adhesive tape.

I worked at the tape on her face then pulled out the paper and went to work on her hands. "What happened?"

The nurse cleared her throat. "Two nurses came by with some charts." She rubbed her wrists. "One of them walked behind me and hit me on the head with something. When I woke up, I was in here."

"Did you recognize her? Was she wearing an ID tag?"

"I've never seen her before, but that's not unusual." She bent over and peeled the tape from her ankles. "There are probably thirty nurses working here that I don't know."

I helped the nurse up and held on to her until she could stand alone. Her name tag said Mason. "Do you remember her name?"

"I think it said St. John or St. Joan. Saint something." The nurse rubbed the side of her head and almost fell backwards.

Taking her arm, I helped her back to the nurse's station. After she was seated, I picked up the phone from the floor and asked to speak with hospital security.

I told them to look for a nurse wearing a name tag with St. James on it and, if they found her, to hold her for the police. Next call was to the emergency room for someone to come up and take care of Ms. Mason.

"Do you remember anything about them?"

The nurse ran her fingers through her hair and looked puzzled. "They just looked like nurses." She flexed her fingers as if trying to reestablish circulation. "There was one thing. One of them was wearing a really awful perfume."

I stayed with her until help arrived then went back to Max's room. I looked at the IV. It looked like the one it had replaced except for the orange tint. The label read 5% Saline. The bottom edge was peeling up and I could tell that it had been glued on by hand. I left that for the police.

"Max. Max." I picked up his hand and rubbed the back of it. "Can you hear me? Move. Grunt. Squeeze my hand. Do something."

His eyelashes fluttered. His breathing seemed more strained than before the IV was changed. He had dark circles under his eyes and the bluish skin around his mouth made him look like an octogenarian.

I called the operator and told her to get emergency personnel up to room 640.

"You should contact the nurse on the floor," answered the disembodied voice.

"The nurse has been attacked and no one is able to answer the call light."

"Have you called security?"

Usually I can tolerate ignorance, incompetence, and a moderate amount of stupidity. Not today. "I HAVE called the police, hospital security, and the emergency room. I have done my part. Now YOU get some help up here."

"Okay, okay!" she replied. "You didn't need to yell."

Throwing down the receiver, I turned back to Max. His breathing was shallow and his skin felt clammy.

****

"Hey!" the deputy shouted. "You can't go in there."

"Get out of the way," a different voice growled.

Hustling across the room, I opened the door far enough to see a hospital security badge on the man at the door. I eased the door open the rest of the way, my Smith and Wesson at my side. Safety off. Cocked.

"Wait in the hall," I eased off the hammer. "Police and emergency personnel are on the way." I threw the deputy a hard look. "Make sure they have appropriate identification this time."

"Yes, ma'am."

Hurried footsteps pounded down the hall.

"Show me your identification." The deputy's voice sounded an octave higher than unusual.

"Get out of the way." Liam sounded like a snarling bear.

"I can't. That woman in there will shoot me if I let you in without seeing your ID."

Liam strode in, pushing his ID case in to his pocket, breathing hard, his face red. He stopped at the foot of Max's bed. "How is he?"

"I'm not sure," I said quietly, not wanting to upset Max. "I yanked out the IV as soon as I saw it wasn't like the other one." I eased the hammer down and pushed my gun back under Max's pillow.

"We need to have that analyzed as soon as possible." Liam walked around, peering in the bathroom, under the bed, and out the windows.

"Looking for monsters?" I settled back in my spot beside the head of Max's bed.

Liam ignored me and kept pacing around the room. He paused at the sound of footsteps in the hall. I could hear the deputy requesting identification.

"That's Dr. Westfall and Nurse Harris from the emergency room." The security guard told the deputy.

The doctor followed by a nurse pushing a cart full of equipment came in. The nurse started checking Max's vitals as the doctor looked at his bleeding arm.

"Did he pull out the IV?" he asked.

"I pulled it out when I noticed the color of the liquid."

"What's wrong with it?" Dr. Westfall turned it so he could read the label. "It's five percent saline. His chart indicates that he is supposed to get it for another 24 hours." He stepped back and signaled for the nurse to take over. "Get that started again."

"You can't do that." I reached across for Max's arm, pulling it away from her.

The doctor pushed my hand away. "You need to step away and let us do our jobs."

"You can't use that IV. It needs to be analyzed."

The doctor shook his head and rolled his eyes. I could tell he was used to having his orders followed without question. "In your professional opinion, just what do you think is wrong with this IV?"

If all went well and my stars aligned just right, I would never be taken care of by this Dr. Perfect. I preferred to be treated like a regular human not a hormone-driven female with a moldy brain.

"The first IV was clear liquid. This one is cloudy and slightly orange." I used my slow, talking-to-a mental-defective voice. "The woman who changed the bag was an imposter."

The doctor leaned back and stared at me. "And how do we know that?"

"She wore my name on her ID tag."

The nurse poked through the cart and pulled out a new IV setup and a unit of saline. I moved away so she could work with Max's other arm. When she watched me pick up my gun and holster it, she sucked in air and started to raise her hands.

"It's okay." I assured her. "I was hired to guard Max."

Liam pulled an evidence bag from his pocket and sealed the contaminated IV bag and tube in it. He called for a crime scene tech to come and pick up the bag for an analysis of the fluid and to check for fingerprints.

When the doctor stopped writing on his IPad, I asked how Max was doing.

"Are you a family member?"

"No." Once again I was butting up against HIPPA. Granted patients need their privacy, but sometimes life would be so much easier if health information was available to anyone interested in it. "I am his fiancée."

Liam snickered. Max's eyes tracked toward me, his mouth quirked.

"I'll be able to answer that question when I see the lab report on the IV fluid. By then, perhaps one of Mr. Ciardi's relatives will have shown up. Miss Harris will stay with him until we get some answers." He closed the iPad and stalked out.

Chapter 11

The investigation of the tainted IV could be carried on without me. Liam would update me when something happened. I needed to get back to my life and Caroline Rand Gardiner. I had ignored the case while Max was recuperating from his knife wounds, and the visit from Liam's ex-wife had set his recovery back. Now he would have to be moved to a safer location.

I had avoided my apartment since the day Max was stabbed. The walls and floor should have been cleaned by now, but the odor of blood still lingered in my mind. Every time I closed my eyes, I saw Max's bloody body.

Mail had stacked up in my letterbox since the last time I was in the building. I pulled out an armload and thumbed through the ads until I found a letter from Duke, Smith, and Holmes, Attorneys at Law. The velum envelope was an exquisite example of the printer's art. Anything looking that official should be framed rather than opened. The last time I received one of these, it was an invitation to a how-to-become-a-millionaire seminar.

I ripped into the envelope as I walked down the hall to my apartment. It was a confirmation of the meeting with Jesse Duke, the attorney for the Gardiner estate. This would be the first time I could meet with him since Caroline hired me to look into her death.

My sofa had been pulled out into the hall with two paint-speckled chairs stacked on it. The filing cabinet sat on the other side of the open door. I heard the growl of cleaning equipment. The landlord was a cheapskate. He would want the building super to clean the blood and paint out of the carpet instead of replacing it.

The red splotches on the walls had been painted over. Not the entire room, just the spots. The institutional beige walls looked like a Jackson Pollock painting. I followed the noise into the bedroom where Ivan was working on the bloodstained carpet.

"Do you think all of that'll come out?" I shouted over the slurping noise.

Ivan shut off the machine and mopped his brow. "It doesn't look like it."

"Why not replace it?" I asked.

"Mr. Wilson wants to save it, if possible." Ivan squatted to look under the bed. "The blood ran under the bed and soaked in. I don't think cleaning will help."

"Perhaps he will just want to cut out the damaged parts." I tried to keep a straight face. "The pad will stink if it isn't replaced, too."

Ivan nodded.

"I'll leave you to your work. I want to pick up some clothes" This was the longest conversation we'd had since I moved in seven years ago.

I looked in the closet hoping that there were some clothes without paint spots. Mandy had dribbled paint across everything on the hangers. I found some clothes in the dresser that she had missed and stuffed them into my carryall.

The handle on the small safe was covered with the red paint. Liam had made fun of me for locking my current files and tax records in it. Now I had a good argument for the next time he commented on my odd behavior. He thought it made more sense to put money in the safe instead of the bottom drawer of my desk.

I twirled the dial to the combination and heard a click, but the handle wouldn't move. I tried to use my multitool to chip the paint off, but the blade slipped every time I poked at it.

"Let me do that." Ivan had been watching me and knew I was more likely to stab myself than remove any paint. "There's already enough blood on the carpet."

"Thanks," I said after he opened the door. I picked up the Gardiner case file and sat on the floor to read through it.

****

The law office, an acre of dark mahogany coordinated with gilded wall coverings, looked like it was designed to both impress and intimidate. The receptionist, clad in a pale-yellow Donna Karan suit, looked as if she had been purchased with the décor.

"May I help you?" Her voice had that rare quality of sounding breathless while projecting to all corners of the room.

"I'm Aggie St. James." I answered in the same breathy tones. "I have an appointment with Jesse Duke."

She wrinkled her alabaster forehead. "I'll let him know you're here."

I wandered over to the floor length windows and stared out over the city until I heard a well-modulated voice call my name.

"It's good to meet you." Jesse Duke extended his hand as if he was expecting me to kiss it. He was a tall, silver-headed man, clad in a navy pinstriped suit. His necktie exactly matched his cobalt blue eyes.

He indicated for me to walk with him down the wide hall. Portraits of people I presumed to be past and present partners, stared out at me, their eyes following my every step. Most of the doors were closed. When we reached the third one, he opened it and stepped back, allowing me to precede him into the office.

Duke gestured for me to take the chair across from the glass-topped table that served as his desk. "You told me Caroline hired you. Can you tell me how you became acquainted with her?"

I began with her telephone call and ended with meeting the deputy she had been engaged to. He listened carefully and interrupted with an occasional question. He asked to see the note.

"The police have the original locked up as evidence." I pulled a copy out of my file and pushed it across the table. "They also have the money she had enclosed with the note."

He punched a number into his phone. "Come in here." Jesse handed the note to the woman and told her to copy it. "How are you paying for the investigation?"

"Out of my own pocket so far. I'm collecting receipts."

"I'll arrange for your reimbursement and whatever your fees are."

Thank goodness. "I'd appreciate it. Do you want me to wait until this investigation is resolved and then present you with a bill or would you like to settle up weekly?"

"It would be best to wait, if that'll work for you." He opened the folder in front of him. "We have received some news about the Gardiner case."

"Is that going to help determine who murdered them?"

"Not really." He drew a piece of paper from the folder in front of him. It looked like hotel stationery.

"We received a holographic will that Ronald Gardiner wrote while they were in New Mexico.

"Can a handwritten will stand up in court?"

"Yes. We were able to confirm the signatures and the validity of the witnesses. Of course, some of his relatives might try to challenge it."

"What are their chances of success?"

"Not good." He leaned back and pulled on his ear. "This is a community property state and she would be entitled to half of everything he owned. Any court case would automatically give her half of his total assets."

"Other than the percentage of Gardiner Electric and the house, what else is in the estate?"

"He had a large stock portfolio, some oil and gas leases, and some miscellaneous parcels of land. Those are to go to other family members."

"This might not help Caroline, but will her family come in for a bigger haul?"

"Probably. This whole matter would have been easier if we had received this document days ago rather than yesterday." He cleared his throat and bit his lower lip, as if searching for the right words. "The staff at the hotel were supposed to mail it when it was written, but they put it aside and found it days later."

"After meeting some of the people who worked there, I'm sure they were waiting for a tip." I recalled the ancient bellhop's act with the dollar bill. "Who inherits?"

"Thirty-nine percent of Gardiner Electric is owned by various investors. Some miscellaneous properties and oil stock are to go to his brother and some cousins. Ronald left the house, its contents, and his Gardiner Electric stock to Caroline.

"That's going to present some problems," I said as I opened my notebook. "His brother has taken liberties with the house. When I went out there, a woman named Margo Baca opened the door. I asked why she was there when Caroline had told me she had been fired. She said Mr. Samuel Gardiner had hired her back."

"Hmm." He looked like he had bitten into a green persimmon. "When was this?"

"The day after Caroline was murdered."

"Was that the first time you met the Baca woman?"

"Yes," I said turning a page in my notebook. "I returned with two police officers and she wasn't there. According to the police, the house was sealed the day they were notified of the Caroline Gardiner's death. We went through the entire house and found no one, but virtually all of the furnishings had been removed."

He poked through the folder and brought out a stapled sheaf of papers. "We have a complete inventory of the house that Ronald had filed with his insurance company. We'll give a copy of this to the police. Hopefully, they can recover the property."

"And find out who took it," I added. "May I have a copy of that list? It might be helpful if I knew more about what was taken from the mansion."

"A copy will be waiting for you at the receptionist's desk when you leave." He called for the woman who had copied the note.

"I tracked down Caroline's family in Needles.

Have they been in touch with you?"

"Yes, her parents are supposed to come in for a conference tomorrow. The will has to be probated before we can start the formal transfer of assets."

"They're probably too proud to mention how poor they are." I stopped to think about what I said. "I mean it looked like they were stretching their income to cover the necessities with little left over for luxuries like travel. You might consider advancing them money for the trip."

"That's not a problem," he said as he closed the folder and stood up extending his hand. "Thank you for coming today. If you don't mind, I would like to be kept up to date with your investigation."

I left thinking about the Rands. They lost a daughter and won the lottery. They had no idea how much their lives were going to change.

Chapter 12

Follow the money. I don't know who said that first, but it sounded like a good place to start. Samuel Gardiner seemed to be the most likely person to know who stripped everything of value from Ronald and Caroline's home. From the size of the house, it must have taken a team of movers to empty it so quickly.

No one answered the number listed for his home. When I called the Gardiner Electric offices, I was told he was on vacation.

"Can you tell me how to contact him?"

"We aren't permitted to give out information on our executives." The crisp, professional voice sounded like a recording.

"I need to talk with him concerning his brother's death. Is there anyone available that I can speak with?"

"Leave your name and contact information on Mr. Gardiner's voice mail," she said. From the number of clicks, my message was at the end of long queue.

My GPS directed me to Samuel Gardiner's house. It was modest compared to Ronald's house. The wood and stone two-storied craftsman stood like a monolith to Gardiner's importance in a neighborhood of single-story ranch houses. It was impressive if not misplaced.

After the third ring, a gray-haired woman answered the door.

"I wondered where you went," I said to Margo Baca, the elusive housekeeper.

"What do you want?" She didn't seem to be happy to see me.

"I'm looking for Samuel Gardiner."

"He's not here." She spoke through the storm door.

"Where can I find him?" I tried to open the door, but it was locked.

"I don't know and, if I did, you would be the last person I would tell." Margo slammed the door and left me staring at the blue-stained wood.

Margo Baca had information I needed to figure out who killed Caroline Gardiner. She must have witnessed the disappearance of the butler and the other unexplained events at the Gardiner mansion. She might have been the one who tried to kill Caroline and ended up poisoning the kitten.

Now Margo was a person of interest in the disappearance and disposal of the mansion furnishings. I would contact the lawyer and let him notify the police. He had all the necessary documentation for a search warrant. The theft of the mansion's contents had to be connected to the murders of the Gardiners.

The most useful person to know is a nosey neighbor. I started with the house west of Samuel Gardiner's. No one answered so I moved on to the houses across the street. I struck gold at the third house.

"I'm Aggie St. James." I handed the shrunken, white-haired woman who answered the door one of my cards. "I'm looking for information about the people who live in the large stone house. Do you know them?"

"Yes, indeedie. I know the Gardiners."

Motioning for me to come in, she stepped slowly

through the entryway and led me past family portraits that had turned sepia with age. An unseen dog growled until it was told to be quiet.

The faded velvet chairs in the living room had crocheted antimacassars on the backs and arms. A huge ginger tabby slept between vases of silk flowers. I could see dust motes and cat hair floating in the sunbeam from the picture window that overlooked the street. The woman sat in a well-used chair with a basket of knitting beside it and indicated for me to take the one facing her.

"I'm Susan O'Neill. Would you like a cup of tea?"

"No, thank you." It wouldn't do for me to tell her I can't stand hot tea. "Have you noticed any unusual activity at the Gardiner's house lately?"

"Well, you understand that I don't neighbor with them. They aren't friendly."

She reached for a cup and slurped her tea. "Are you sure I can't get you some tea?"

I just shook my head.

"About a week or so ago I thought they were moving out because a huge truck pulled up in front of their garage and stayed there for two, or was it three, days? On the second day, I saw some men around it. So I put on my shawl, took my dog Sadie, and walked down to the corner and back. They were carrying furniture into the garage. Some of it looked rather nice."

A big black and white cat hopped up into my lap and dug his claws into my leg.

"Never mind Wally. You're sitting in his chair."

I patted his head, then encouraged him to get off me. "He's a big one," I said, rubbing the claw marks where he had landed. "Did you talk to anyone about the furniture in the truck?"

"I spoke to one of the gentlemen. He told me I needed to ask the Gardiners. He had a Mexican accent and I had trouble understanding him. But neither Samuel nor his wife was there so I came home."

"Did you see where they were putting the furniture?"

"I did take a peek and it looked like they were stacking it in the garage. That's a terrible way to treat such nice things."

"Have you seen anyone taking items out of the garage?"

Ms. O'Neill reached down and scratched Wally's back. "I'm trying to remember. One day last week, maybe Tuesday or Wednesday, not as late as Thursday, I saw a van backed up to their garage. It said Olde Towne Antiques on the side."

I thanked her and stood to leave. "You have my card. Please call me if you notice anything else happening at the Gardiner's house." I tried to get out before Wally noticed and the dog started barking.

Thank God for nosey neighbors.

****

I slid my seat back as far as possible, laid the binoculars on my lap, and pulled out the latest John Connolly novel. I planned to watch Samuel Gardiner's house until it was time to babysit Max.

I tried to slog through *Every Dead Thing* while I waited for something to happen. If I hadn't paid for the book, I would have thrown it away after the discovery of hundreds of dead children. That kind of storyline always dampened my enthusiasm for a book. Reading it in the middle of the day with the sun shining was the only way to stave off the nightmares.

My ringing phone gave me an excuse to put the book aside. "St. James Investigations."

"I need a private eye." The voice sounded young and a little reticent.

"How can I help you?"

"Well, this is a little personal and a lot embarrassing." She hesitated and cleared her throat. "I'm not sure I can talk about this with a stranger."

"If you can't tell me what you need, I can't be of service." I heard a whisper in the background. "You need to speak louder."

"Um. It's like this." She raised her voice a couple of notches. "I was at a party last night."

She paused for several seconds so I prodded her along. "And?"

"I was with my boyfriend and we were drinking and then we went parking at the lake."

"Let me guess, you lost your virginity and you want it back."

I could hear snickering as I hung up on her. She sounded a little young to be making crank calls. At least she gave me a break from that book.

I continued watching the Gardiner's house. Other than a delivery truck dropping off packages, nothing moved except the leaves on the trees. After the truck rounded the corner, a rust-riddled van pulled up to the first house. A man stepped out and walked casually to the house and picked up the package the delivery man left on the stoop then he crossed the lawn to the second house and picked up another. I could see more packages through the van's front window.

I dialed 911. "I'm watching a porch pirate in action

on Bravado Place." I identified myself and gave her the van's license number and its description.

She said a car was already on the way. "Is he still there?"

"He has another package to pick up and then I suppose he'll be moving on."

A squad car skidded around the corner and parked in front of the van. The driver fired up the engine and threw it in reverse. When the officer pulled out his gun, the driver killed the engine and put up his hands.

People drifted out of the houses from up and down the block. They gathered around the police car, asking questions while peering in the van's windows.

Susan O'Neill waved as she strolled by with her dog. Liam would have loved seeing the two of them. He always commented on how dogs look like their owners. Ms. O'Neill's butt matched her corgi's as they waddled past.

The officer locked the van driver in the back of his squad car, then spent a few minutes talking to the gathering.

"I need that package he picked up at my house," said the woman from the first house.

"Sorry." The officer handed her a card. "You can call that number and they will tell you how reclaim the package."

"Why can't you just give it to me?" She pointed at the package on the front seat. "It's right there."

"Everything in the van needs to be booked in as evidence. The lawyers will argue for a while." He reached over and slammed the van door. "When they agree to use photos in court, the packages will be released."

"That's irritating." The woman rolled her eyes and the rest of the gathering agreed with her.

The officer shrugged. "That's the law."

When the crowd dispersed, I introduced myself to the officer. A wrecker pulled up to the van as the cop took down my information.

"You sure got here fast. I only had time to hang up before you skidded around the corner."

"You had been noticed. We received a call about a woman looking into houses with binoculars." The officer put his notebook in a pocket. "What are you doing here in this neighborhood?"

"I was hired to do some snooping."

"What kind of snooping?"

"I'm looking for the man who lives in the house with the blue door. Who called and reported me?"

"I wasn't given a name. The caller was afraid you were scouting around for a house to break into." He hitched up his pants and spat on the grass. "You need to move along."

Chapter 13

Max had been moved to the security ward in the top floor of the hospital with the rest of the miscreants and crazies. Lab tests showed a lethal dose of iodine in the IV. If it had continued to drip into his arm, it would have stopped his heart. I had pulled it out before he received enough to kill him.

I showed two forms of picture ID, had my picture taken, and forked over my revolver before being admitted to the security ward. A repeat performance with the IDs finally got me into Max's room. Thank goodness the deputy had been replaced by officers who looked competent and wide awake.

"How is he?" I asked Liam. He was tightening his tie and pulling on his sports coat. I noticed his empty holster and felt better. Even police officers don't get special gun privileges here.

"Better." He picked up his crossword. "The doctor said he might be able to get out by the end of the week. If Mandy has been caught, he can go back to his apartment. If not, we'll have to find him a safe house."

"It seems like Max is safe here. Do you still want me to stay with him?"

"Yes. I don't want him left alone." He stood staring at Max, chewing on his lower lip. "By the way, Kathy Garber dropped by and left that bag for you." He pointed to a plain paper sack on the floor by the bed.

"What's in it?"

"I didn't look."

I kicked off my shoes and opened the bag. It was the paint-smeared wooden box from my closet. I held it up and tried to open it. Kathy had promised not to open it and I guessed the guard at the entrance to this floor didn't chip off the paint to see what it contained.

Liam held out a hand. "You need some help opening it?"

"No." I settled in the hard plastic chair. "That would be like opening Pandora's box." Some memories are better left locked up. "Do you want me to finish that crossword for you?"

Liam was territorial about his puzzles. "What do you think?" he said sticking it under his arm as he left.

****

I pulled out a *Guns and Ammo* magazine from my tote bag. I continued reading aloud the article about the Army and Marines use of the Barrett MRAD sniper rifle that I had started the day before.

A raspy voice interrupted me before I could finish the first paragraph. "What are you doing?"

Max stared at me, his eyes half-closed. His face had some color in it and the five-day beard made him look like a sleepy pirate.

"Exactly what I have done every night since you ended up in here." I put the magazine on the bedside table. "You liked hearing my voice."

"Only because I was unconscious."

The old Max was back. "Liam said you are going to be thrown out of here Friday. Have you figured out where you will be staying if Mandy is still running

113

loose?"

"My sister stopped by this morning and wants me to stay with her." He wriggled around trying to sit up. "She lives in a zoo with her husband, three children, my mother, two dogs, and a canary. She doesn't have room for me unless I want to sleep under the back porch."

I handed him the bed controls. "Use this." I pulled up his pillows and straightened the bedding. "Are you comfortable or do you want me to call a nurse?"

"You can go away now. I don't need a babysitter."

"Tough."

I settled back in the chair and reopened my magazine. With Max awake, this looked like it was going to be a long night. He and I have never had a pleasant conversation since the day we met.

****

Jesse Duke was excited about locating of some of the Gardener's furniture. He emailed me a longer list of the stolen items. This one came with a brief description of each and where it was located in the mansion. He said he would work on a search warrant for the house on Bravado Place.

I went back to Liam's condo and crashed for a couple of hours. Hobo and I shared breakfast as I looked over the email. I made a list of some furniture I wanted to buy at the Olde Towne Antiques. Or at least that was what I was going to tell them. I pulled on the only paint-free clothes I owned and hoped they wouldn't notice the red dots on my loafers.

The antiques store was near China Town in a building that looked older than the Golden Gate Bridge. The front, scarred by peeling paint, had faded gang graffiti over much of it. Some of the windows were covered with plywood and others encrusted with grime. A sandwich sign on the sidewalk announced that the store was open on Wednesday and Friday afternoons.

I checked to see if I had a full clip in my gun and texted my location to Liam. Like an anxious parent looking after the slow-witted child, he insisted on knowing where to start looking if I disappeared,

The door protested as I pushed into the store. The lighting was dim except for an area in the back. I peered around looking for a salesperson, but it seemed I was the only person in the store. I walked slowly toward the light, listening for any sound that would indicate I was not alone. An old, scarred desk held untidy piles of papers, an old rotatory phone, and a bell. I tapped the bell and waited.

"Who's there?" A watery voice asked after my third ring.

"A customer." I replied with my hand on my gun.

The man tottered toward me, dragging one foot, leaning on a cane. His face looked like a map with the roads marked in gray and the lines around his eyes were red. His clothes were old and clean. They hung on his frame as if he had lost a lot of weight.

"What can I do for you?"

"I'm looking for a Louis XIV living room sofa and matching chair."

He looked at me and shook his head. "We don't have anything like that. Mostly we have used American furniture."

"Have you ever carried Renaissance paintings?"

"No." He shook his head. "We don't handle art works."

This wasn't what I expected. I believed Susan

O'Neill saw the Gardiner furniture in Samuel's garage as some of it was loaded into the van. Margo Baca had to be involved somehow. But who else could have helped her? She didn't look strong enough to clear out a mansion by herself.

"My mistake. I was told that you had a shipment of rather nice antiques two or three days ago."

The old man scratched his scraggly beard and looked up as if expecting an answer to drop out of the air. "Are you sure you have the right business?"

"Some men were seen taking furniture from a garage and loading it into a van with your store's name and location on the side."

"Oh, I sold that van to a nice young man last month."

"Do you have his name?"

"No." He shook his head again. "It was on the check, but I cashed it the day he gave it to me. I wanted to make sure it cleared the bank. In fact, I took it to the bank it was written on, the First Western of California. You can't be too careful."

"Can you describe the man?"

"Well." He nodded and looked back at the ceiling with one eye closed. "He was sorta young and he had black hair and a Mexican accent. It wasn't real noticeable, like he could speak it, but had grown up here. He had a funny last name."

"Was it Baca?"

The old man looked thoughtful, nodded. "Yes. I believe it was."

"I appreciate your help." I handed him one of my cards. "If you hear from that man again, please give me a call."

It was coming together. Perhaps the Baca I met in New Mexico was a relative of Margo. This was the link I needed to follow and, if I was right, it could lead to the murderers of Ronald and Caroline Gardiner.

****

I stopped by Jesse Duke's office to tell him about the missing van and driver. He was interested in the witness who saw the Gardiner's furniture being loaded into it.

"Susan O'Neill lives across from the Gardiners. She walked over to see what was going on and saw two men moving nice furniture into the garage." I didn't mention that she was incredibly nosey.

"We may need to contact her about what she observed."

As he wrote down the description of the van and the license number, his pen scratching was the only sound in the room. "Will the witness be willing to testify in court if she is needed?"

"No doubt." I thought she was the embodiment of neighborhood watch. Nothing missed her attention and she seemed willing to tell all she knew. Susan O'Neill would be thrilled to become involved.

"I'll have an associate take a statement from her so we can get a search warrant for that garage."

"You might want to include the house and any outbuildings," I added. "There was a lot of furniture taken from the mansion. Will the police assist in locating the van?"

"Yes," he said as he rose from his desk. "Once we get the search warrant, we will have a county deputy go with us to serve it and we will have the police look for the van."

He held the door open, letting me know it was time for me to leave. His secretary hustled over to escort me out. She walked me all the way to the elevators. I have been thrown out of several places, but never as quickly or nicely. If she weren't a secretary, she could get a job as a bouncer.

Chapter 14

"Do you think your apartment is safe?" I asked as Liam stopped stirring his coffee to erase a word. There were so many black smudges littering the page, that his daily crossword looked as if a chicken had stepped in ink and walked all over it.

"Max refuses to leave the city, so it's as safe as anywhere we could find."

I reached for a donut from the box on his desk.

"Put a dollar in the cup. Those aren't free."

I bit into the donut then put it back in the box. "Just how long have you had these?"

"No more than a week or two."

I have never seen Liam eat a donut. He thought they were the work of the devil when he was a child and his opinion has become more intrenched with the passing years. I asked him why he bothered to buy donuts since he doesn't eat them. He said the chief wants all upper-echelon officers to look hospitable when anyone enters their offices. So, Liam chose coffee and donuts. He told me he buys a dozen and keeps them until they are gone, and then he buys more. At first, they disappeared in a couple of days. Now that the rest of staff knows how stale they are, a dozen will last a month or more.

"How are you going to keep Mandy from finding

out where you're stashing him?" I sipped the coffee and reach for the creamer. "Is it safe to put Max where Mandy can find him?"

"We're hoping she tries to get at him again." He put his puzzle down and refilled his cup. He held the pot toward me and I put a hand over my cup. Liam's coffee was almost as bad as his donuts. "You and I will take turns staying in the apartment while undercover men surround the building. If she shows up, we'll be ready."

"Does he know he'll be locked up with your cat for an indefinite time?"

"I talked to Hobo and he agreed to leave Max alone."

"Am I still doing the night shift?"

"Yeah. I'll relieve you at six after I get off work." Liam got up and stretched. "By the way, how are you doing with the Gardiner case?"

I brought him up to date on the furniture discovery and the two Bacas. It didn't sound like a lot of progress, but I hoped finding the furniture was the breaking point of the case.

****

"I don't need a babysitter," Max growled as I held the door for him. He wore a gray sweatshirt with San Francisco Police Academy across the chest. It had been white when he got it during his training. His black sweatpants were ripped over one knee and paint stained. He shuffled in, slightly bent over, holding a hand over his stomach.

Liam offered Max his arm. "I'm going to put you to bed before I leave you in Aggie's capable hands."

Max waved it off and sat down on the living room

sofa. "Just leave my bag in the bedroom and take her with you." He pointed at me.

"You two need to try to get along until Mandy has been corralled. There's food in the kitchen and your medicine is on the table," Liam opened the refrigerator. "Who put this crap in here?"

"That's my food and don't you dare throw it out." I pushed him away and closed the door. "I can't live on roots and tree bark like you do."

"It's your life." He pulled on his jacket. "Just don't try to poison Max with that garbage."

Hobo came out from under the table and rubbed against my leg. I scratched his ears and put some kibble in his bowl.

I gave Max a bag of Hobo's favorite treats. "This is how you get along with the cat. Liam feeds Hobo the same kind of food he eats. A few of these treats and you'll own him."

"You sure?" He turned to the back panel of the package.

Max and Hobo have been at odds for years. Hobo won most of the battles with a hiss and a slash. Max hated cats, and Hobo must have sensed it. Max had told Liam that a wild cat had attacked him when he was in elementary school and he still had nightmares about it. Most of his scars had faded except the ones covered by his hair and the white line above his eyebrow.

"Do you want to sleep on the couch or the bed?"

"What kind of babysitter goes to sleep while she is on watch?" Max looked like he was about to fall asleep, too.

"The kind who hasn't slept for about a week." I opened my case and took out a robe and pajamas.

"Hobo will wake me up if anything happens."

****

A rusty growl startled me awake. When I moved to get up, Hobo leapt onto my stomach. The absolute darkness left me momentarily disoriented. The lights were off inside the apartment and there was no ambient light from the street.

"What's going on?" Max asked in a stage whisper. "Why are the lights out?"

"Get down, Hobo." I pushed him off and tried the lamp switch. "I don't know, but the electricity is off outside, too."

I stumbled across the room and pulled a flashlight from my purse. A quiet rubbing sound disturbed the darkness. It came from the front door. I flashed the light around the room and focused it on the door locks. With my gun in hand, I tiptoed to the window beside the door and moved the curtain aside. A dark figure stood with his back to the door, a gun visible in the moonlight.

When Liam's number went to voice mail, I called 911. I identified myself and gave the address. "The electricity is off and we need an officer to come over now."

"No electricity is not an emergency." The disembodied voice lisped into my ear. "You need to hang up and wait for the lights to go back on."

"I have a recovering police officer here whose life has been threatened. I need help now." I wanted to scream at the woman but I knew from past experience, when you got loud, they either lose your call or spend ten minutes explaining the proper use of the 911 service.

"I am transferring your call to the duty officer."

I went to look in on Max and check the windows in the bedroom. Hobo had joined him on the bed. They were eying each other suspiciously. Hobo looked ready to strike. As weak as Max was, he probably shouldn't make any sudden moves.

"There's someone standing outside the door. I've called for an officer. Until help arrives, I want you two to try to get along." His service revolver lay beside his hand. "You aren't allowed to shoot the cat."

Either Max or Hobo growled at me, I couldn't tell which. I crept back to the front door and looked out the window again. The shadowy figure had not moved.

A police car pulled up to the curb and spotlighted the figure by the door. The man held up a badge case and waved at the cruiser. The officer walked up to the door and knocked. "Ms. St. James."

I opened the door and invited him in. "Thank you for coming so quickly. I heard some scratching noises and saw this man outside the door."

"Officer Byers is one of the undercover officers watching the apartment."

"I didn't mean to scare you," the officer said. "We couldn't see with the lights out, so I came over to stand in front of the door."

If I hadn't been so tired, I would have been embarrassed for being scared. With Mandy on the loose, I wasn't willing to take a chance of her surprising us.

"Were you scratching on the door?"

"I was leaning on the door," Byers said. "I was trying to be quiet, but I guess I wasn't as successful as I thought."

"How's Max doing?" the other officer asked.

"You can go and see for yourself." I pointed toward the bedroom. "He's in there having a staring contest with the cat."

Chapter 15

"Can you meet me at the Gardiner mansion?"

"Yes. When do you want to go there?"

"Two this afternoon, if it is convenient." Jesse Duke added that it was time to bring the family up to date on the investigation. "The Rand family hasn't seen the property nor been told about the missing furnishings yet."

I arrived early and sat on the front steps waiting for everyone to show up. The lawn smelled like newly-mown grass and the shrubs had been weeded and trimmed. It looked nice, but I would've planted a few marigolds among the boxwoods and arborvitae. The broken second-floor window had been replaced. The new glass glistened and made the rest of the windows look dirty. I hoped the interior was cleaner than the last time I saw it.

A Sprinter van followed a maroon Lincoln up the drive. I stood and watched the younger Rand children scramble out of the van and stare at the house. The side door opened and a ramp slid out. Harley Rand waited for his son's wheelchair, then guided it to where the rest of the family stood. Emily stepped beside her husband and looked up at the house. Amazement and disbelief flashed across her face.

"The door in the rear of the house enters directly

into the kitchen and it has no steps." Jesse herded the family along the drive toward the back entrance. "We hired a gardening service for the lawn and a pool company to clean and make necessary repairs to the pool and gazebo. We have a cleaning service that we can recommend for the interior of the house. Of course, you can make any changes you wish."

Emily had the shocked look of a woman staring at a ghastly car wreck. "This is a bit overwhelming."

"Dad." Sam and Eric, the ten-year-old twins, raced up. "Can we go swimming? Our bathing suits are in the van."

"Not now," Harley said. "We want to see the rest of the property first."

Jesse led them onto the patio and fished a handful of keys from his briefcase. All of them were tagged except a massive skeleton key. He sorted them out on a small wrought iron table.

"We had all the locks in the house changed as a safety precaution." He pushed the skeleton key toward Mike. "This one operates the elevator. The key is an antique and would be almost impossible to replace."

Jesse unlocked the door and stood aside for them to enter. "The interior is going to be little rough until the cleaning service gets here."

"Holy cow!" Claire exclaimed, turning circles in the kitchen. "This is huge!"

A little rough was an understatement. The house was redolent of disuse and dust with a mild overtone of mildew. The floors needed cleaning and some refinishing. I guessed the furniture thieves scratched the woodwork when they moved everything out. Dust patterns showed where the furniture and the pictures used to be.

Voices echoed through the empty house as the children raced from floor to floor to see it all. One of the girls staked her claim on a bedroom and another declared that she was older and got to choose first.

Caroline's parents just stood trying to take it all in. I watched them look around the entryway, then they turned toward Jesse and me.

"Was this really Caroline's house?" Emily asked. Her voice had a slight quiver in it. "How could that be?"

"Yes," Jesse said. "Caroline inherited the estate when her husband was murdered. This is all yours now."

"When can we move in?" Harley pushed open the French doors and peered into the empty formal living room.

"You signed all the necessary papers when you were in the office. You'll probably want to wait until the cleaning service finishes." Jesse handed them a folder. "One day soon, we hope to return the original furnishings that were illegally removed. Some of them have been located and we have initiated legal actions to recover them."

"This is hard to believe," Emily said. "We didn't know Caroline was married. And to a rich man at that."

"Caroline wasn't married long before her husband was murdered," I said. "We're still looking into that as well as her death."

Guiding Harley and Emily into the kitchen, Jesse gestured for them to sit in the breakfast nook. The high-backed benches built into the wall looked like the privacy booths in French restaurants. The cushions were missing. Perhaps they would be found with the furniture recovered from the house on Bravado Lane.

The doors on the commercial-sized refrigerator were propped open. I could see a few containers that looked like mold factories. The massive range needed a good going over. The stove was half the size of my kitchen, but Emily would no doubt put it to good use. The appliances must be tough to sell. There probably wasn't a lot of money in used kitchen appliances.

"We want to know where Caroline is and when we can have a funeral." Harley took his wife's hand and gave it a squeeze. He reached in his pocket and handed her a handkerchief as if on cue. She dabbed her eyes.

"The coroner has both bodies now and will release them for burial as soon as the autopsies are complete. Caroline was shot, but the cause of Ronald's death was less obvious," I explained. "He was exposed to a substance that has yet to be identified."

"Will the Gardiner family take care of his funeral services?"

"I don't think so." I was thinking of his relatives' perfidy. "His brother and cousins might be in jail and unable to attend."

Jesse pointed at the folder in Harley's hand. "Those are the names and numbers of the services we hired to help with the house. You need to call the security company and have them change the alarm codes."

"All this must cost an awful lot of money," said Emily. Her brow wrinkled with concern. "I don't know how we can afford all this."

They had signed the transfer papers, yet they had not absorbed the extent of their fortune. The Gardiner Electric company accountants would lay it all out for them when the will and the other documents were finalized.

"I don't think that's a problem." Jesse closed his briefcase with a snap of the lock. "The company has deposited three hundred thousand in the account we opened in your names. Your debit cards are in the folder. If you need extras, just call the controller."

"What did you say?" Emily rattled a finger in her ear. "Say again."

"How can that be?" Harley tilted his head toward Jesse. "Are you sure?"

I enjoyed watching them learn about their newfound wealth. If you can call it that. Jesse chuckled and I joined in. With all that had gone wrong in the past days, it was fun to watch the Rands try to comprehend their new reality.

"You're quite wealthy now," I said.

They just looked at each other; Harley shaking his head and Emily sniffling. After years of stretching every dollar until the eagle screamed, it would take time for them to learn how to handle their newly acquired wealth and the responsibilities that came with it.

Jesse and I watched them peer around the room. Their faces had the slack look of people left standing on the corner watching the last bus of the day pass by.

The two girls thundered down the back staircase, shattering the silence. "Can we stay here tonight?" yelled Kim, the twelve-year old.

Eight-year-old Claire pushed in front of her. "We picked out our bedrooms and we want to stay in them."

"Just a minute, girls," their father placed his hands on their shoulders. "I don't know if we can."

"You can move in any time you wish, but the

furniture won't be here until the police release it," Jesse explained. "You might want to see what you have before you do any heavy-duty shopping."

"But Dad," Kim whined, "we brought our camping gear to save money on hotel bills."

"Yeah," Claire added. "We can camp here."

"We have reserved a residential apartment near here if you change your minds." Jesse gave them directions and a brochure. "All of the utilities are on if you choose to stay here."

Harley told the girls to go find their brothers and bring them to the kitchen. They scampered off as loudly as they came.

"We'll stay here tonight," said Emily, "but I need to do some grocery shopping."

"I can help you with that." I pulled a city map from my purse. "There's one more thing. If anyone, man or woman, named Baca comes to the house, don't open the door. Call 911 immediately."

"Uh. Is there something you haven't told us?" asked Harley.

"Well." I took a moment to figure out how much they needed to know. "Juan Baca and his Aunt Margo were in on the theft of the furniture from this house. They may also have been parties to the murder of Caroline and her husband Ronald."

"But I don't think you are in any danger," Jesse interrupted. "Just get the alarm taken care of today."

"Do you have any idea when the police will release the furniture?" Emily paced into the vacant entry and traced over the dusty outline where a picture had been hung.

"We have a clerk working on it right now." He

nodded goodbye to the Rands then walked me to my car.

The traffic had lessened with the setting sun. Now that the Rand family was settled in their empty mansion, my next step would be to track down the Bacas. They kept popping up in unexpected places and I needed some answers.

When I took the offramp leading to Liam's apartment, I noticed a van coming up behind me. Its left headlight was pointed to the side as if it had been in an accident. The color was indistinguishable in the twilight, but I thought it was a light color, maybe white. I stopped at the light and the van eased into the lane two cars behind me. I turned to the north and the van followed.

Perhaps I was being paranoid, but I had the feeling that I was being tailed. I had seen a white van twice on my way to the Gardener mansion. Now here was another one, or perhaps it was the same van.

I veered into the right lane and slowed down to let it pass. Another car came between us, honking repeatedly, so I sped up and turned into a taco stand. I circled the parking lot, then cut through the traffic and headed south.

"Do you have someone following me?" I asked Liam when I was sure the van had disappeared.

"No," he replied. "What makes you think you picked up a tail?"

I told him about spotting the van on the freeway. "It followed me when I pulled off the highway."

"Are you sure?"

"The left headlight was out of alignment." I watched my rearview mirror for the follower.

Liam mentioned that I might want to go to the police station. "The Stolen Property Squad has retrieved some of the furniture and artwork from Samuel Gardiner's house. There was so much, it won't fit in the Property Room."

The law firm representing Ronald and Caroline was working to get some of the furniture released to the Rands, but everything had to be logged in for future litigation.

Jesse Duke's law clerk was checking the confiscated items against the Gardiner's insurance list. His ill-fitting suit and bow tie indicated his rank in the law firm's hierarchy. Every time a piece of furniture was moved, he admonished the police officers to not scratch, dent or drop it.

"Yah, we know." The gravel-voiced cop growled after the third time. "If you'll step out of the way, we can get this finished and then we can all go home."

The clerk pursed his lips and moved back half a step. He looked like he was going to argue but the cop held up his hand and motioned him to keep backing up. The clerk slowly walked backward until he was in the hall.

"When can this be moved back to the mansion?" I asked the clerk.

"That's up to the court. We are asking that the furniture be released now and the artwork can be held for evidence. We're at the mercy of the judicial system."

****

No lights shone through the windows of Liam's apartment. I let myself in and called out, "It's me, Aggie."

Hobo came out of the bedroom, stopping to stretch and yawn. I turned on the lamp and gave him a scratch. He rubbed around my ankles and yowled loudly.

"Are you hungry?" I followed him into the kitchen. His bowl was empty and his litter box was full. I poured out his crunchies and replaced the litter.

"Hey," Max called from dark bedroom, "bring me something to drink."

I took a bottle of water from the fridge and went in to see him. He lay on top of the covers with his pajama shirt open. The bandage on his stomach had traces of dried blood around the edges. Max had replaced the pajama pants with a pair of Liam's cargo shorts.

"Do you want to take a shower before I change that bandage?" I handed him the water bottle.

"What makes you think I need a bath?" Being stabbed hadn't improved his temperament.

"You smell like Hobo's litter box." I straightened his pillows and covers, then I cleared away the burger wrappers and donut bags that were strewn across the bed. I picked up his prescription bottle from the floor. "Do you need to take one of these now?"

"Later." He groaned as he tried to push himself up higher on the bed. "I want to watch the football game before one of those knocks me out."

I collected the gauze pads and antibiotic ointment from the bathroom along with a wet washcloth and told him to slide over so I could sit on the side of the bed.

"What do you think you are going to do?"

"Your bandage needs changing." I lined up everything on the nightstand.

"The nurse will take care of it tomorrow," he snapped. "You need to go away."

"What nurse?"

"The one the hospital scheduled for me." He pulled his shirt over the bandage.

"That's odd." I didn't think the hospital was told where Max would be taken to recuperate. "Who called you?"

Max pushed a dirty coffee cup aside and handed me a note. It was difficult to read through the brown splotches.

"I need to check this with Liam." I reached for my phone. "There's something wrong here."

Liam told me to bring the cop in from the squad car in the street and stay away from the windows until he could check it out. "Max isn't scheduled for home health care."

"Are you going to be here to greet the nurse?"

"You'll have to handle it this time." I could hear him shuffling papers. "I have to testify in court this morning and I can't get it changed."

"Have you explained about Max?"

"It didn't help. This trial has been postponed three times and the judge is getting grumpy."

"And we don't want to cross Judge Grumpy." I walked in to the bedroom. "I'll give him the bad news."

"What?" Max snarled.

"There is no nurse in your future."

I pulled Max's shirt open. "Either I change this now or I call an ambulance and have you hauled back to the hospital and they can do it." The best way to deal with Max was to ignore his wishes. "Well? Which is it?"

Most people stepped away when Max scowled at them. I just smiled and reached for the bandage. I eased it off his stomach, cleaned the dried blood, and recovered it.

"See there. It didn't hurt at all." I handed him a stale donut from the nightstand. "Here's your reward for being a good boy."

The donut sailed past my ear as I went to the kitchen. Max was getting better every day.

Chapter 16

Sergeant Ted Watson stood like a statue, his dusky skin and navy sweats blended in with the night. Liam had asked him to help keep an eye on Max while we waited for the nurse to show up. Ted had planned to spend his vacation trying to catch a record muskie in Minnesota, but he delayed his trip to help keep Max alive. He took the first watch.

I relieved him as dawn lightened the sky. Nothing had disturbed the night. Waiting for the mystery nurse ramped up the stress with every passing hour. I must have jumped a foot when the newspaper hit the door.

"What was that?" asked Ted from the darkened room. He had stretched out in the recliner.

"The newspaper," I muttered. "You need to get some sleep."

"Maybe later," he said.

The sleeping pill I'd given Max at midnight would not wear off for a few hours. With luck, he would sleep through whatever was going to happen. I was pretty sure Mandy was the nurse we were waiting for. The question was how she planned to get at Max.

The note Max gave me had said she would be here at ten. I watched the clock hands mark the minutes so slowly time seemed to stop. I checked my cell and asked Ted what time he had. The wall clock was doing its job.

"You need to relax," said Ted. He had resumed his place by the door. "We have a man on the roof across the street. He'll let us know if anyone comes to the door."

Ten o'clock came and went without a nurse. The sergeant's relief arrived at noon. Ted checked the peephole, then opened the door. A woman officer stepped in and introduced herself as Twyla Baxter.

"I'll leave it with you." Ted pulled on his jacket before stepping out the door.

As soon as he closed the door, I immediately knew something was wrong. Her uniform was too long and had a dark stain on the right side of the jacket. She had not removed her hat when she came through the door as we were taught at the academy. And her perfume….

Mandy had changed. The blonde wig had slid around until the ear piece was in front of her ear. She had always had perfect make-up, but now her eyebrows needed shaping and her mascara had oozed down her cheek. Lines radiated around her eyes. She appeared defeated until I looked in her eyes. A shiver ran up my back at the insanity that flashed there.

"May I see your ID?" I asked. She snapped it open and shoved back in her pocket so quickly I couldn't read it. "Can we do that slower? I want to read it."

Instead of her ID, she pulled a Glock from her holster. "I have been waiting years for this day." Her voice rasped as if she hadn't used it for a long time. "Call Liam. I want him to watch you die before I kill him."

"Where did you get the uniform?" I asked. I had punched Liam's number as soon as I smelled her. She always wore patchouli. It reeked. I was sure she hasn't had a mosquito bite since she was in elementary school.

I pretended to punch in Liam's number.

"From the moron across the street. If you must know."

"Is that blood on the front of that uniform?" I asked, hoping Liam was listening and would send help. "Did you stab the officer?"

A knife had always been Mandy's favorite weapon any time she thought someone had crossed her. The gun was new.

"Had to," she said. "He would've called here and I couldn't fulfill my mission."

"I assume that's his gun."

Sidling toward the kitchen, I forced her to turn her back to the bedroom. I wanted to keep her talking to give Liam time to send help and warn Max if he woke up. "What mission was that?"

"Liam destroyed my face. He has to pay for these scars." Her voice grew louder with every syllable.

I squinted at her face and stepped back again leading her farther away from Max. "I don't see any scars." Two more steps and I could reach the messenger bag I left on the kitchen table.

"Are you blind." A drop of spittle ran down her chin. "They are right here." Mandy pointed to the lower part of her face and neck. Her gun hand trembled.

I heard a rustle of cloth from the bedroom, so faint I almost missed it. Mandy's head snapped up. "What was that?"

"Probably the cat." I stepped nearer the table. "Hobo always sleeps on Liam's bed." I wanted to keep her away from Max. If he was awake, he might still be too groggy to defend himself. The more time I could give him, the clearer his thinking would be.

"I killed that cat," she glanced quickly around the room. "Did he get another one?"

"You didn't kill him," I said. "You just cut off a couple inches of his tail." Hobo was crouched behind Mandy, ready to attack, his truncated tail twitching.

"Where is he? I'll shoot him first."

"I thought you always used a knife," I said trying to keep her attention on me. As long as she kept talking, she wouldn't be shooting Max or the cat.

She nodded toward the window. "It got stuck in that cop's neck, so I took his gun."

"Have you ever fired a Glock?"

"How difficult can it be if every lousy cop and gangbanger in town can use one."

Thank goodness Liam never took her to the range. She probably wouldn't be able to kill us, but I still didn't like the odds. She might get lucky.

The soft scrape of a footstep in the bedroom warned me that Max was out of bed. I hoped he had his weapon ready because Mandy was losing patience with me. I grabbed for my bag.

"Stop!" Mandy fired a shot in my direction. Her hand shook so violently the bullet punched a hole in the refrigerator.

I seized the handle of my Smith and Wesson. Before I could pull it out, the next shot grazed my arm.

Hobo hissed. Mandy swung around and, before I could grab her arm, she fired just as the cat flew at her. She screamed when his claws dug into her arm.

I kicked the gun out of her hand as Max stepped out of the bedroom, his Glock leveled at her.

Ignoring the pain in my arm, I tried to subdue Mandy, but she punched me in the eye and dove for her gun. I grabbed her ankle, yanked her to the floor. Max stepped over and toed her gun under the couch.

She kicked me in the face with her other foot. I let go of her ankle and latched onto one of her flailing arms. She screamed when I thrust it up as far as I could behind her back while she swore at Hobo. She reached back and tore at my hair with her free hand while thrashing around trying to throw me off her back. I grabbed her other arm and forced her over onto her face with both hands pinned as far up as I could push them. Her feet hammered on my back.

Hobo bounded across the floor and leapt onto Mandy's head. She screamed when he dug his claws into her scalp, his tail swishing in my face.

"Move over, Hobo." I tried to get him out of the way. "Max, get the cuffs out of my bag."

Max clamped a cuff on one arm while I tried to hold the other one still. Once the other cuff was snapped on, I jumped away. She continued spewing venom and thrashing until she rolled against the door. Her diatribe against Liam and me was impressive.

A key turned in the lock. The door opened a couple of inches. "Let me in," Liam shouted. He pushed on the door but Mandy was lying against it.

I resisted the temptation to drag her across the room by her hair. But I pulled her away from the door with one of her feet. When he stepped over her, she spat at him and swore through clenched teeth.

Liam saw the blood oozing from my arm and the swollen eye. "Are you all right, Aggie?"

"I will be when you get her out of here." I wrapped

some ice cubes in a dish cloth and held it to my eye. "I need a couple of pain killers. It feels like she ripped out most of my hair." I reached down and scratched the cat behind his ears. "Hobo, you're the hero of the hour."

Max eased onto the couch, holding his stomach with one hand. His face was ashen and blood seeped through his bandage. He took the clip out of his gun and put both pieces on the cushion beside him.

"Do you need an ambulance?" I asked.

Max shook his head and leaned back. "I just need a minute. You look worse than I feel."

Two officers arrived to take Mandy into custody. She fought the manacles, spitting and biting one of the men before they could put a spit mask on her and chain her hands at her waist. The shackles on her ankles limited her ability to kick out at anyone but they didn't stop her from jerking around.

"Time out!" I pulled off the hat. "You need to look your best for your mug shot." I yanked her wig so the ear piece was in the middle of her forehead and slapped the hat on her head. "There you go."

"I'm coming back and kill all of you!" Mandy screamed through the spit guard on her face.

Liam held the door open. "Don't take those restraints off her until she's chained to a hospital bed."

Mandy twisted back and forth trying the buck off the officers. She was still screaming profanities as they led her out of the apartment.

Liam reached for a bottle of bourbon on the shelf above the refrigerator. He pointed to the bullet holes. The one that grazed my arm struck slightly higher than the first. "Who?"

"Mandy," said Max. Then he pointed toward a

small hole in the floor. "She missed the cat, too."

Liam poured a double shot and held out the bottle to us.

Chapter 17

"Are you moving out?" I watched Max shuffle around the room packing his belongings in a grocery bag. His progress was so slow and jerky that I wanted to push him aside and finish the task.

We had left Max to his own devices since Mandy was locked up with the rest of the criminally insane. I had stopped in to check on him on my way to the police impound lot. "Do you need help with your packing?"

"Don't you have something better to do?" He dropped a bottle of pills. We watched it roll across the living room floor until Hobo raced in and gave it a whack. "Dammit cat! Leave that alone!"

I grabbed the bottle before Hobo could bat it under the sofa. Max growled at the cat and Hobo hissed at me. I dropped the pills into the bag and checked the bedroom for more of his things. A pair of house shoes along with some socks and underwear were under the bed.

"Did you miss these?" I held out the items I collected.

Max nodded. He turned toward the kitchen and stumbled. I caught his arm and guided him to the recliner. His skin was grayish and sweat beaded on his forehead.

"Are you sure you're ready to take care of

yourself?" I retrieved a bottle of water from the fridge. "Drink this."

He popped up the footrest. "Let me sit for a few minutes and then I'll be ready to go."

His voice was so weak I barely heard him. I watched his eyes close. When he began snoring, I tossed a blanket over him and called Liam.

Mandy had trashed Max's second-floor apartment as she did mine without the splattered paint. His sister was setting it in order, but there was no elevator. He was getting stronger, but stairs would be too much for him.

"Max thinks he's leaving," I told Liam. "He packed his things in a paper bag and is taking a nap now."

"Just let him sleep. I'll be out of this meeting in an hour."

I could hear an electronic voice droning in the background. It sounded like one of the chief's pet training videos I used to sleep through.

"What's the subject this time?"

"The history of the Miranda and Escobedo court cases and their ramifications for the modern police force." Liam yawned and cleared his throat. "You want to join me?"

"No, thanks. I know everything I need to know about those court cases from the 1960s." I watched Max sleep with Hobo curled up between his ankles. "The parking cops located Juan Baca's van and I need to take a look in it before he can get it out of the impound lot."

"Go ahead. I'll look after Max."

I had days when everything went my way. The car started without the fan belt screeching, traffic moved at just the right speed so I could get to the office without having to stop at every light, and an interesting case waited to be solved. But that wasn't today. There was a massive traffic jam when a truck spilled a load of mattresses on the freeway, followed by a flat tire as soon as I drove down the offramp. I pulled into a tire store and, after an hour and a handful of cash, I was back on the road. I had just enough time to get to the impound lot before the office closed.

I handed the clerk the van's license tag number and my credentials. "I need to look at a van that was impounded today."

"How did you know it's here?" The woman asked without looking up. She wore a bilious green uniform that was so tight she appeared to be testing the strength of seam and fabric. A pair of half glasses was perched on the end of her nose.

"The police called me when it was located."

"Do you have a release?" She nudged her glasses up. I watched as they oozed back to the end of her nose. "Well? Where's your paperwork?"

"I don't want to take the van." I watched her push her glasses up again. "I just need to look in it."

"Come back when you have the proper paperwork." She pushed my credentials through the window and yelled, "Next."

I stepped aside, slotting my ID back in my wallet when a man rushed up to the counter. He thrust some papers toward the clerk. I glanced at his reflection in the glass cage. His scruffy beard needed trimming and his clothes should have been washed last week. He exuded that body odor that reaches up and yanks out your nose hairs. Still, he looked like someone I had met before. I could not remember where.

Shave the facial hair and run him through a carwash, he would look a lot like Juan Baca. I resisted the urge to hold my nose and I stepped closer to listen as he spoke with the clerk. He was reclaiming a van that had been impounded earlier in the day. When I heard him read off the tag number, I checked my notes then hustled out to my car and waited. That was the tag number on the old furniture van.

When Baca came out of the building, an attendant pointed to where he was to wait. I moved my car and backed into a space near the entrance. Before I could text Liam that I had found Juan Baca, the van pulled up and the attendant handed over the keys. Baca motored past me and turned south toward Highway 80. The van had the same misaligned headlight as the one that followed me from the Gardiner's residence.

I pulled in behind him, eased off the gas to allow a car to move between us. He took the freeway east into Oakland, where the evening rush hour was in full swing. Traffic moved too slowly for the exhaust fumes to dissipate. Running the air conditioner kept me from passing out, but my eyes watered and my nose ran at full speed. But at least I didn't need to worry about losing the van as the traffic inched along.

A half hour later Baca took the Grand Avenue exit. I followed him southeast past a shopping center into an industrial area. This must have been a prosperous area until the people and businesses moved on. The entrance, modeled after the Brandenburg Gate, was decorated with bullet holes. Piles of plaster shards were scattered among the straggly weeds. Plywood covered the windows of an Asian buffet and a defunct Sears. A small tailor's shop shared a space with a dry-cleaning business.

The few remaining stores had barred windows and doors. A dollar store stood in regal splendor in the middle of acres of cracked concrete. The cars parked near it were as dilapidated as the buildings. Every flat surface was tagged with graffiti.

The van switched lanes so quickly that I blew past it just as he disappeared into the Wilson and Company Storage premises. I continued driving until I found a restaurant parking lot where I could turn around.

The storage facility covered several acres. The sun sat low on the horizon as I pulled in the drive. I proceeded to the right and drove around several rows of buildings. Baca's van was parked in front of one of the large storage rooms at the back of the lot.

Parking at the end of the row, I got out and closed the door quietly. I peered around the corner of the building and watched some men carry a sofa out of the van. When they disappeared through the door, I moved up behind a rusted-out Chrysler and watched the men move more furniture into the storage room. Still too far away to identify anyone, I crept closer as they carried in a dresser and stopped in the recessed area between a wall and a door.

Their voices drifted on the cooling air, but they were speaking Spanish too quickly for me to understand. My three years of high school language classes failed me. I strained to figure out what they were saying when the ominous ratchet of a shotgun shattered the air.

"Don't turn around," a voice growled behind me. "Put your hands behind your head and start walking." I felt a cold steel barrel against my back.

Taking a quick look behind me, I started toward the van. I had been so intent on what the men were saying, I had forgotten to watch for Juan Baca.

The men watched us walk toward them. My first inclination was to scream but, since there were no other people in sight, it would have been a waste of breath.

"Move." He yanked the messenger bag off my shoulder. Now he had my ID and gun, but I still had my phone unless he checked my pockets.

He kept the shotgun in my back until we walked into the storage room. Furniture was stacked half way to the ceiling with only a small open area near the overhead door. In the glare of the bare light bulb, I could see that the furniture was high end and probably antique.

Baca handed the shotgun to one of the men. "Watch her." He took out my wallet and went through the contents. He dropped everything on the floor except my ID. "Well, we meet again, Ms. St. James. I thought I got rid of you in New Mexico."

"I'm still looking for answers." I stared at him.

The smarmy Lothario I had met in the Wingate Police Station hadn't made it to California. The man holding the gun looked like the cop who manhandled me out of the police station in New Mexico. "Is this your fellow officer?"

Baca let out a hoot of laughter. "What do you think?" He pointed at the other man. "Diego, check her pockets."

He yanked off my jacket and found the phone along with an assortment of tissues, coins, and lint. "Turn your pant pockets inside out."

I did as I was told. Breath mints and my gas card hit the floor. Baca gestured for me to turn around so they could see I was harboring a gun in the waistband of my jeans. People had died at the hands of these men. I was careful to move slowly and obey their instructions. They had all the advantages.

Baca took the shotgun back and pushed me aside so the two men could continue unloading the van. They carried in a dining table and stacked chairs on it. An armoire was the last piece of furniture unloaded.

"Now, we get to deal with you," said Baca as one of the men pulled down the overhead door. The ceiling light cast ominous shadows in the storage room.

Time for answers was short and I had better hurry. "Before you do that, I have a few questions. Did you kill the Gardiners?" I tried to sound curious rather than accusatory.

"What's it to you?"

"I was hired by Caroline to find her killer." I needed to choose my words carefully. "Do you know why she died?"

He took down one of the dining chairs and told me to sit. "I might as well tell you since you won't be leaving here." He told the men to tie me to the chair.

"We don't have a rope." Diego looked around. "What do you want us to use?"

"Figure it out."

I watched as they tore the damask covering on a settee into strips. The antique sofa went from mega bucks to worthless trash in seconds. Diego tied my hands behind me and another man fastened my ankles to the chair legs.

I had read in a magic book that if you tensed your

wrist muscles when you were being tied up, you could loosen the ties. When they finished, I relaxed my arms and felt the ties were a little looser, but not enough to free my hands.

"We were bagging heroin in the attic in their house. We had a good thing going until that butler saw Diego crossing the lawn late one night and followed him. He told the Gardiners about finding food in the attic and they started asking questions. When they fired Margo, they had to go."

That must have been the missing butler Caroline mentioned. "What did you do with the butler?"

"He's in the bay feeding the fish." Just saying that brought a smile to Baca's face. "It was easier to get rid of him than the others."

"Why was there food in the attic? How did it get there?" I was stalling for time, hoping to find a way out of this mess. I needed for him to keep talking.

He relaxed against the table, his ankles crossed. "Margo brought meals up when we had a batch to work. It was the dishes not food that caught the butler's attention."

"How are you related to Margo?"

"My mother's sister," he chortled. "She'd been working in that house for years. After the police raided the warehouse where we had been packaging the drugs, I needed somewhere new. She cleared a place in the attic in exchange for a percentage of the take."

I wondered about the price of loyalty. "How much did you pay her?" The Gardiners should have been able to trust their housekeeper. After all, she was privy to all their secrets.

"Not a lot."

"Why did you kill the Gardiners?" I asked. I strained to loosen the ties around my wrists. I could feel them slip, but not enough.

"When Margo was fired, she went to Samuel Gardiner for a job. He'd hated his brother because their father left the business to him. He saw a way to grab the company as well as all of Ronald's other assets." Baca's voice sharpened and color stained his cheeks. "It would have worked if he hadn't married that damn secretary."

"Why did that matter?"

"You ever heard of community property? We had to get rid of her so Samuel could inherit it all."

"Let's get back to Ronald's death." This is the one thing I hadn't figured out. Caroline said she heard a hiss just before Ronald fell over dead. "What caused him to die so quickly?"

"It was a lot easier to get rid of him than his wife. All I needed was some bee venom and one of those automatic sprayers like they use in the army." He looked proud of his ingenuity. "Anaphylactic shock was my best friend. It worked really fast."

"He was allergic to bee stings?" I could feel the ties start to stretch.

"He almost died twice from stings when he was a kid." Baca stepped away from the table. He pocketed my phone and ID. It looked like he was getting ready to leave.

"So, were you responsible for all of Caroline's accidents before she died?"

"The bitch lived a charmed life." He spoke through clinched teeth. "When pushing her under that bus didn't work, I had to track her down and shoot her." He pushed the door up and signaled the other two men to precede him.

Diego looked at his watch. "We need to meet that buyer in fifteen minutes. He wants a bunch of this furniture"

"Let's go." Baca looked back at me. "I'll be back later to deal with you."

"Where are you going?" I asked. I worked at the ties around my wrists. They were looser, but not slack enough to pull one of my hands free. "Are you just leaving me here?"

"Oh. I'll be back." Baca let out a bark of laughter. "Count on it."

The men's voices were cut off when the van doors slammed. The starter growled and the motor sputtered and died. It took two more tries to keep it running. The driver revved the motor and the van chugged away.

Chapter 18

Watery sunlight shone through the cracks around the slats in the door. The dim light bulb cast shadows on the walls. I kept working at the fabric ties around my wrists. The cloth had been torn from a period settee that looked like it had been covered with wool over horse hair padding. My wrists were chaffed and I could feel blood oozing over my hands. The material was slowly stretching. Perhaps the blood weakened it.

My right hand came loose first and the tie fell off the other. I pulled the strips of cloth from my ankles and looked around for something to use as bandages. I looked through the contents of my messenger bag that were scattered across the floor and found couple of tissues to dab at the blood on my wrists. Then I collected the rest of it and shoved it back into my bag. Everything seemed to be there except the keys Baca had taken along with my ID, gun, and phone.

I pawed through desk drawers hoping for a first aid kit, but all I found were receipts, pens, paper clips. All the scraps someone would toss in a desk.

The chairs and tables stacked toward the back of the room were what you would find in a parlor or studio, but no drawers, cabinets, or shelves. As I clambered over the sofa Baca's man had cut up, I looked down and found my salvation, perhaps.

A multitool lay on the floor, the knife blade open. I crawled behind the sofa and retrieved it. Someone would want his Leatherman back and, hopefully, he would return for it sooner rather than later.

I looked at the rolling steel door. It was constructed by slipping the slats into the frame and screwed into the bracing on the sides. The braces were bolted to the bottom and top of the frame. All I had to do was take out the screws and bolts.

Leatherman advertisements claimed it would handle any job around the house or car. They were optimistic. There wasn't a blade for bolts and the screwdriver looked a little small for the job.

I tried each of the screws. Two of them were loose, but the rest might take more muscle than I possessed. I worked at the screws until I loosened a few on one side. King Kong couldn't have removed any of the others.

Between swearing and grunting, I felt another one move when a car stopped outside the storage room. I heard the motor quit turning over and a door slammed. I grabbed my messenger bag and squeezed in the corner by the door.

I heard slurred words.

"I'll be right back." Footsteps came closer. Metal clattered against the door. "Come over here with that light. I can't see the keyhole."

I clutched the Leatherman, its largest blade open. My breathing slowed as my heart beat like a maniacal drummer.

After what felt like an hour listening to them fumble with the lock, the door slid up slowly.

"I know I left it here this afternoon," the man caught his toe on the threshold and stumbled into the room.

His partner with the light followed him. He was walking better, but they both reeked of alcohol.

When they shuffled toward the butchered settee, I stepped out the door, grabbed the handle, and slammed it down. The lock was hanging in the metal loop with the key sticking in it.

"What the hell?" One of the men banged on the door, trying to raise it.

I stood on the handle and fastened the hasp over the loop and snapped the padlock in place.

"Let us outta here," one of them bellowed and beat on the door.

I waited until they ran down. "It's your turn to figure out how to get out of there."

"You can't leave us here."

"Turnabout's fair play," I shouted through the door. "I'll send someone for you. Maybe."

I left them yelling and beating on the door while I went through their car. I found a phone with a dead battery and I took their keys in case they figured a way out of the storage room. I pocketed the cell phone and threw the keys as far as I could into the weeds.

My car was where I parked it. Juan Baca had my keys as well as my ID. Fortunately I kept an emergency key under the front bumper.

The business office was closed. I hadn't spent enough time in Oakland to know the city so I drove to the restaurant where I had turned around earlier.

The Sunnyside Diner looked like family affair. The heady aroma of fried chicken with an undertone of burned coffee permeated the air. The walls were covered with grease-stained prints of bygone days and an iron gate that spelled out Sunnyside framed the entrance to the kitchen. A cashier, dressed in a mustard yellow t-shirt with the diner's name emblazoned across her massive bosom and green knee-length shorts, offered me a menu. "Welcome. May I show you to a seat?"

"No, thank you," I replied. "Could I use your phone?"

"We don't allow customers to make calls on our phone. Sorry." She managed a look of insincere regret. "We must keep it open for call-in orders."

"I need to call the police." I handed the menu back to her. "My phone was stolen, but I can pay you for the phone call." I pulled out my wallet and offered her a five-dollar bill. The money disappeared in a move that any magician would envy.

"Right this way." She indicated a phone on the hostess podium. "Please keep it short."

I thought Liam might know someone in the Oakland PD who would be helpful. When my call went to voice mail, I was stuck with 911.

"What's the nature of the emergency?" The 911 operator asked in a nasal monotone.

"I have located some stolen furniture in a unit in the Wilson and Company Storage on Grand Avenue."

"Stolen furniture is not an emergency."

"I agree." I crossed my eyes and breathed deeply. Number one on my bucket list was never speak to another 911 operator. Every time I spoke with one of them, my blood pressure spiked enough for me to feel my heart pound in my ears. We could never communicate in English, and it was the only language I knew.

"Calling this number when there is no emergency is a violation of California state law."

"Yes, but the two thieves I left locked in the storeroom might disagree with you."

"One moment." A buzz followed by several clicks came down the line.

"I am the supervisor," said a man with a slight Middle Eastern accent. "Miss Turner has reported a misuse of the emergency call system."

I explained who I was and why I called. When he finished interrogating me, he agreed to send a patrol car to meet me at the storeroom.

"Since this is not a true emergency, it may be a while before one can meet you."

I took a couple deep breaths and pictured yanking that twit through the phone line by his nose. Perhaps in the future that would be possible.

I asked the cashier who let me use the phone if I could get a cheeseburger and fries to go. I needed to get back to the storage company to meet the police. If a miracle was in the works, they might show up this week.

The sodium vapor lights cast a muted glow on the lot and I could see no other cars in front of the storeroom. I didn't know if Juan Baca might come back. Without my revolver, I didn't want to run into him.

Parked in the shadows at the end of the row of storerooms, I pulled the cell phone from my pocket and checked to see if I had a charger that would work with it. The last car charger I purchased came with five different-shaped plugs. The fourth one I tried fit. Now, if the phone would take a charge, I might be able to communicate with the world again.

Waiting reminded me of all the times I had been hired to watch wandering spouses. Surveillance was the least favorite facet of my job. I ate my dinner and watched for the police. Then I picked up the floating scraps of paper, empty cans, and fast-food wrappers off the floor and stuffed them into the burger bag.

When all was tidy, I sat staring at the cell phone. Waiting for it to charge was as interesting as watching cement harden. I propped it on the dash so I could keep one eye on the storeroom. Counting the moths buzzing around the overhead lights helped keep me awake.

Twenty-seven moths later the cell phone showed a slight charge. I tapped in Liam's number at one minute past midnight, his usual quitting time. With the luck I'd had today, he would be working overtime.

He finally answered the third time I called. "Alexander."

"It's me." I spoke through a yawn.

"Whose phone are you using?"

"It's a long story and it can wait. Do you know anyone in the Oakland Police Department?"

"If you want me to help you, I want the short version."

It gets harder and harder to find good help. "I followed Juan Baca to his storeroom, got caught, tied up, locked in, got out, locked two of the thugs in, called 911, and have waited for three hours for the cops to show up." I stopped for a breath. "Can you call him now?"

Chapter 19

When the Oakland Police car stopped in front of the storage building, I pulled up and parked next to it. The spotlight that had been shining on the roll-up door swung around and lit my car like the sun. I blinked until I could focus on the tall officer with a hand on his gun.

I rolled my window down and put my key on the roof and clutched the steering wheel with both hands. "My ID and license were stolen, but I have my car registration in the glove box."

"Let's see it." His voice rumbled like it was a struggle to speak. If I could have seen his eyes, I would have been able to judge his mood. Wearing sun glasses at midnight seemed questionable, but I chose not to ask why.

"Two men are locked in there." I nodded toward the storeroom. "If we're lucky, they'll have passed out by now." I fumbled through the flotsam that had accumulated since I acquired the car. I handed him the registration folder along with my insurance card.

"Okay, little lady, why are they locked in there?" He read the papers while his partner walked up beside my car.

The pair looked like Mutt and Jeff. The short cop pulled off his sunglasses and cleared his throat. I could imagine that he wanted to slap his leg with a crop and demand that I drop to the ground and do fifty pushups. He acted like the movie stereotype of a drill instructor.

"It's a long story." I unlocked the door and started to push it open.

"Don't get out of the car." The short partner closed the door before I could put my foot out. "We need to check for wants and warrants."

While one of the officers typed my information into the computer, a pickup pulled in. Rust and mud obscured the original paint color which might have been blue. Black exhaust belched out when he turned off the motor. While the engine shuddered and died, the driver threw out a burning cigarette butt and cleared his throat.

He sounded like he was trying to hack up a porcupine as he climbed out of his truck. His clothes were filthy and his boots were covered with something that might have come from a barnyard. He ran his hand over his thee-day-old beard and focused on me.

"You Aggie St. James?"

"Yes," I replied, "and you are?"

"Lou Herman." He croaked.

"You a policeman?"

"Yeah. You Liam Alexander's girlfriend?"

"Just a friend," I said. "Did he tell you what happened?"

"No. He just said I owed him and to get down here."

"I'm glad I'm not the only one he keeps score on. What is he holding over your head?"

"It's another long story." He scratched his stomach and cleared his throat again. "Suffice it to say he bailed me out of a lawsuit."

My life is full of long stories. I have always been nosy and this sounded too good to pass up. "So what were you being sued for?"

"My ex wanted my hogs."

"Okay." That was enough information to satisfy my interest.

The officer holding my door shut stepped aside while I went through the day's events. I climbed out and pulled the padlock key out of my pocket. "I locked a pair of unhappy drunks in there. I don't think they have guns, otherwise, there would be bullet holes in the door."

He signaled for the officers to stand to the side, then Herman balled up his fist and banged on the door. "Anybody in there?"

"Let us out of here," a distorted voice answered.

"Lie on your stomachs, hands behind your heads," Herman yelled. "There are three guns pointed at you and we'll shoot if you so much as twitch."

"Okay, okay. We'll do anything to get out of here."

The policemen lined up their guns on the door as I removed the padlock and rolled it up.. The men on the floor were a little worse for the wear. The one wearing the yellow shirt looked like he had tried to yank out his hair. The man in the plaid shirt had taken off the jacket he wore the last time I saw him and his clothes looked slept in. The officers cuffed and seated them on the cut-up sofa.

"Do you mind if I ask them a few questions?"

"Sure." Herman yawned and scratched his arm. "Knock yourself out."

"Where is Juan Baca?"

"No hablo English," the one in the plaid shirt said.

"What?" I asked, my voice going up an octave. "English?"

Plaid Shirt shook his head and closed one eye. He was going the have a heck of a hangover tomorrow.

"You had no problem speaking English when I locked you in." I decided to keep the volume up to see if sound might improve his language skills. "Where is Baca?"

Both men shuddered and Yellow Shirt groaned. If they hadn't left me locked in this room, I might have felt sorry for them.

A little louder. "Where can I find Juan Baca and the rest of the furniture you stole from the Gardiner mansion?"

They both flinched and Plaid Shirt shivered like he was sitting on ice.

"I will tell you everything I know if you'll just quit yelling," Yellow Shirt spoke so quietly I had to lean toward him to hear what he was saying. "He lives in an apartment over near Fisherman's Wharf."

"And the furniture?"

"I don't know. We were just hired to empty the van."

He didn't know much, but now I should be able to find Baca. "What about your friend here?" I pointed at Plaid Shirt. "Do you think his English has improved enough to tell me what he knows?"

Plaid Shirt had started snoring while I spoke with Yellow Shirt. His shoulders were hunched over and his head bent toward his chest. He looked even more hungover than his companion.

"Hey!" I yelled at him. Both of them jumped. "What do you know about Juan Baca?"

He coughed and cleared his throat. "*Nada.*"

Plaid Shirt understood enough English to answer the question. Ah, progress. He might be deaf. Perhaps volume helped. "Where did you meet Juan Baca?"

He cringed and crossed his eyes. "Do you have to scream?"

"I'll quit yelling if you answer my questions." I pulled up a chair and sat in front of them. I was feeling the effects of the long day. "Again, where did you meet Juan Baca?"

"We did some work for his aunt last winter." Plaid Shirt closed his eyes and clenched his teeth as if every word clanged in his brain. "She recommended us."

"Did you know the furniture was stolen?"

"He said his aunt was moving and wanted it stored."

I looked at Lou Herman. "What do you think we should do with these guys?"

He stopped scratching his head and turned to the other two cops. "Put 'em in jail for the night. Ms. St. James will come down in the morning to fill out the paperwork."

"What's the charge?" the tall cop asked. He helped Plaid Shirt off the couch and held on to his arm long enough for him to stop weaving back and forth.

"We'll hold them for unlawful imprisonment, trespassing, public drunkenness, and assault until we have straightened this out."

The officers took the men to the squad car. The shorter officer put a hand on Red Shirt's head as he shoehorned him into the sedan. I heard the prisoner moan.

"Those two are going to be so hung over, I feel like

throwing up out of sympathy." Lou rubbed his stomach. "It's going to be a couple of days before they feel human again."

"I've been down that road. I'd pity them if I hadn't been stuck in that room."

I shook his hand. "Thanks for helping. Maybe this will get you off the hook with Liam. Although, he has a memory like a supermax computer when it comes to debts."

"Yep," he answered. "Now you owe me."

****

I was parked in the McDonald's parking lot trying to firm up my schedule for the day while having breakfast. "I need to talk to those two men we hauled out of that building last night."

"What do you want to know?" Lou Herman yawned as if he had just woken up.

I caught myself following suit. Yawning and eating can't be done at the same time so I gulped down the last of my breakfast sandwich. "One of them said he knew where Juan Baca lived over by Fisherman's Wharf." I took a sip of my coffee and almost scalded my mouth. "Ouch!"

"Are you eating breakfast?"

"Maybe," I said fanning my mouth. I had no idea how they could make a cup of coffee that hot. "I need more information so I can find Baca without having to comb through every building in the area."

"If you bring me two sausage biscuits and a large coffee, I'll get you into see them, but you better hurry. Bail hearings start at eleven o'clock and there's no telling where they are on the docket."

"Do I need to go to the jail or the courthouse?"

"The jail," he said with another yawn. "They do video bail hearings."

Since I became self-employed, I have always tried to sleep late enough to avoid the haze that hangs over the city in the early morning. By ten o'clock it would dissipate as the sun burned through, then the smog would take over. If I wanted to speak with Red Shirt and his friend, I had to get on the road with the haze blurring the skyline.

I keyed the address into my GPS. Most of the traffic was headed into San Francisco in the morning, so I would be in Oakland in thirty minutes or less. The cars on the Bay Bridge were running a few miles over the limit until we slowed down for the toll gate.

"Follow I80 to the Nimitz Parkway." The robotic voice was helpful but it was too early to appreciate her dulcet tones. The GPS was wonderful invention designed to take us from here to there without getting lost. But there have been times when I wanted to get even with her, so I keyed in my home address before I took off. Listening to her *"make a safe U-turn at the next left," "return to Elm Street and turn right"* and *"go around the block"* was more entertaining than listening to the news on the radio.

"Take the Market Street Exit and turn left on Seventh Street."

"Go back to sleep." I switched her off as I pulled into the public parking lot across from the jail.

Lou Herman was leaning against the stair railing smoking the stub of a cigar. He was more presentable than last night, but he still looked like he shopped at Goodwill. His suit and shirt looked slept in. The knot in his gray tie was pulled down. If the tie had been covered with flowers, the greenish stain might have passed as a design. I handed him the coffee and breakfast sandwiches. He tossed his cigar into a trash can then motioned for me to follow him into the building.

I emptied my pockets and opened my bag to prove I wasn't armed. The metal detector went off and I checked my pockets again. One of the deputies told me to step aside so he could check me out with a hand-held wand. When he pointed it at my head, it went off again.

"Do you have a metal plate in your head?" he asked.

"No but I have fillings in my teeth." I opened my mouth.

"Teeth won't set this off. Turn around." He waved the wand again. "What's in your hair?"

The silver clip holding my hair back was the culprit. I pulled it off so I could pass inspection. Lou stood drinking his coffee while I stuffed everything back in my pockets. Redoing my hair would have to wait.

We signed the visitors log and waited until Red Shirt was brought in. His name was Jaime Rodriguez.

"Where can I find Juan Baca?" I asked him through the small holes in the plexiglass window that separated us.

"Who's that?"

"The man who hired you to move that stolen furniture."

"Oh, that guy." He shook his head as if to clear out the fog. Jaime eyes were bloodshot and his skin looked yellow. He was so hung over that he would have to get better to die.

"Yes. That guy." I repeated. "Will if help if I speak louder? It seemed to help last night."

He shut his eyes and rubbed his forehead. "If you won't yell at me again, I'll answer your questions."

"Where can I find Juan Baca?" I repeated.

"He was staying in an apartment over one of those weird shops on Haight Street."

"What's the name of the shop?"

"I wasn't paying no attention." His voice trailed off and he propped his head on his hand.

"Try to stay awake for a few more minutes." I rapped on the glass. "What kind of shop was it?" I asked when he straightened up and looked at me.

"Old hippie stuff."

"Clothes? Furniture? Art?"

"Clothes, I think. I was only there once." He shook his head and stared at me like I had fallen out of a spaceship. "I think he lives close to Masonic Street in a second-floor apartment."

"Did you see anything that would identify his building?"

"You have to go up an outside staircase. Juan's apartment is the only one up there."

I thanked Rodriguez and signaled the officer that we were finished. He did add some information. At least I had a starting place.

"Do you need to talk to the other one?" Lou asked.

"No." I pushed my notebook into my bag. "I'll see where this takes me."

Chapter 20

Finding a parking place on Haight Street was almost impossible. I circled the block and held up traffic while I waited for a van to pull away from the curb. I ignored the Prius honking behind me. I headed into the space on van's bumper. If I had parallel parked like that, I would have flunked my driving test. The last and only time I tried to back into parking place, another car beat me to the slot and the driver was out and shopping before I could get the car in reverse.

The temperature was in the high seventies and the air was reasonably clear. I climbed out of my car and stepped into the flow of tourists which allowed me to look around without being obvious.

A woman with long straight hair, no makeup, and Jesus sandals handed me a leaflet that described the area as *funky*. From her flowered skirt and many strands of beads, I agreed. She must have been here since the sixties. I asked if any of the buildings had apartments over them and she told me they all did.

I started at Masonic Street looking for outside stairs. Store windows displayed flower child memorabilia and some the proprietors were in to their seventies. The third clothing store had spiral wrought iron staircase on the side leading to the second floor with a wooden ladder to the roof.

I stood at the counter behind a pair of teenagers who were trying on bangles. The man waiting on them wore a flowered shirt with a string of puka shells and striped bell bottoms. The old hippie flashed a peace sign after he handed back their change.

"Does anyone live in the apartment upstairs?" I asked him when it was my turn.

He peered at me over blue-tinted half glasses. "Yes."

I pulled a picture of Juan Baca from my bag. "Is it this man?"

He held the picture up to the light and squinted at it. "No, I live up there." He pulled off the blue glasses and replaced them with a pair of glasses that were strong enough to double the size of his eyes. "I only wear these when I want to read something." He looked at the picture again. "I've seen this man pass by a lot."

"Do you know where he lives?"

"I saw him go around the corner by the pottery shop over there." He pointed toward a pink and gray building across the street with a narrow alley on the side. 'Why are you looking for him?"

"I'm tracking him down for an inheritance." Once again, I didn't cross my fingers.

I thanked him for his help and joined some women looking for a break in the traffic before jaywalking. We stepped off the curb just as a driver pulled away from a parking space, revved his motor, and honked at us. He flashed us a one-finger salute and disappeared down the street in a fog of half-burned gasoline.

I reached the other side of the road just as the light changed and another line of cars scuttled down the street. I strolled past the building and checked the alley.

There were stairs to the second floor. I peered in the window before I went into the pottery shop.

Hundreds of pots lined the walls. The shelves were set so close together it was difficult to walk through to the sales counter. I peeked in the back room where several people were throwing pots. Some of them were highly skilled. Others threw pots that were lopsided or sliding off their wheels.

A woman in a clay-spattered apron noticed me watching them work. Her blonde-streaked hair looked like it might have started the morning in a tidy bun. Now about half of it had escaped. "Can I interest you in lessons?" She pushed a lock of hair behind her ear.

"No, thank you." Pottery-making is among the artsy-fartsy things I have no patience for. "Is there someone living above your shop?"

"Yes, but Juan told me he'll be moving out at the end of the week. If you're looking for a place, I'll be happy to show it to you."

"Yes, please." I tried to sound blasé, but I was jumping up and down in my mind. This was a piece of luck I never expected.

"I'm Maggie," the woman said as she removed her apron. Her tunic had a maroon splotch across the front that ran down onto her trousers. "I spilled some glaze this morning," she said when she saw me looking at it. She pulled keys from a drawer and led me to the stairs outside of the building.

Would Juan be inside? Is he armed? The metal steps rattled and shimmied with every step we took. I hoped we would make it to the top before the rusty staircase collapsed from age and disrepair.

Maggie knocked on the door and yelled, "Anybody

home?" She pounded on the door again, then turned the key. The door creaked open and she yelled again. When she got no answer, she gestured for me to follow her inside. "Come on in."

The apartment looked as if the tenant was packing to leave before the date he had given Maggie. "Do you mind if I look around?"

"Feel free to look wherever you wish," she said. "He was supposed to give me at least a month's notice."

I walked through the apartment, opening doors, peering into every nook and cranny. A few clothes hung in the closet. In a far corner, I saw a police uniform with a New Mexico State Patrol arm patch. This looked like the shirt Baca had worn when I met him weeks ago.

The drawers and cabinets were empty. I looked in an open box and saw paper plates and plastic tableware, but no cookware.

"Does the refrigerator come with the apartment?" I asked, as an excuse to open it. I found some cheese and sandwich meat on the top shelf that looked edible. The milk jug was swollen and the lettuce was brown.

She nodded as her phone rang. I would have plowed through every box in the house if I had been alone, but Maggie stood in the middle of the living room talking on her cell phone.

A Tiffany lamp and two crystal vases looked like some that were stolen from the Gardiner mansion. Some other glassware was on an end table.

"Do you like the apartment?" Maggie asked as she slipped her phone into her pocket. "You can't beat this location and the rent is reasonable."

"This looks good, but I've an appointment to look

at another this afternoon." I lied.

Maggie had her hand on the door knob when footsteps clattered on the stairs.

"Shush!" I pushed her behind the door. With my Smith and Wesson in my hand, I signaled for her to be quiet. Her eyes widened and she put a shaking hand on my arm. "Be quiet," I whispered.

The door flew open. Juan Baca stepped inside kicking it closed. He carried a fast-food bag in one hand and a large soft drink in the other.

"Juan," I stood behind him, cocking my gun. "Put your hands up!" He slowly raised his hands over his shoulders. "What's going on?"

"I'm making a citizen's arrest and holding you for the cops." I prodded him in the back with my gun forcing him toward a battered straight-backed chair. "Sit. Don't make any sudden movements."

Baca took two steps and threw the soda over his shoulder, splashing it in my face as he juked to his left. I ducked so he couldn't hit me with the food bag as he spun around, crouched with his fists up, one hand holding the sack.

"You ain't taking me anywhere." He kicked my hand and the gun sailed across the room.

I danced away from him. He took a wild swing. I ducked, and before he could try again, I kicked him in his fuzzy lumpkins. He doubled over and I kicked him in the head. He fell face down on the floor.

I straddled him, grabbed his arms, and bent them behind his back. "Get my cuffs out of my purse," I yelled at Maggie.

"What's going on?" Her voice quivered and she rubbed her hands together. "Why are you sitting on him?"

"He's wanted by the police for murder among other things." I tightened my grip on his wrists, shoving his hands farther up toward his head. Baca jerked and thrashed his legs trying to throw me off. "I need those handcuffs now."

Maggie dumped the rubble out of my bag. She searched through it, picked up the bracelets.

"Clamp them on his wrists."

"Uh, do I have to?" Maggie backed toward the door. "I don't know how to do that."

Oh, lord! Why is it so hard to find good help? "Haven't you watched cop shows? All you have to do is clamp them on just like in the movies."

It was all I could do to control Baca. He flailed his legs back and forth, his back and hips wriggled. It was like riding one of those mechanical bulls you find in bars.

"Come on, Maggie. I can't hold this guy forever."

She crept toward us reaching out with the cuffs. She stopped too far away to help.

"You are safe as long as I hold on to him." She still stood frozen. "Come on. You can do it."

Finally, she clamped a manacle on his left wrist. "Will that do?"

"Now just put the other one on."

After I tightened the bracelets and got up, Baca rolled over and tried to lurch to his feet.

"I'm going to kill you for this, you bitch."

I kicked his rump. He landed on his face with a cracking sound. Blood pooled on the floor.

Setting the chair over his torso, I sat long enough to catch my breath. "I'm going to have to hit the gym if I am going to make a habit of this." I signaled to Maggie. "Come and sit here while I make a phone call."

She hesitated halfway across the room. "Are you sure he won't hurt me?"

"You'll be okay." I checked the chair to make sure Baca couldn't move. "It won't take long for the officers to get here."

With Maggie keeping the prisoner in one place, I retrieved my gun and pointed at Baca while I called Liam. He was asleep and didn't sound happy to be called this early. Once I explained that I had Juan Baca in cuffs, he agreed to send someone and told me to wait for them.

"I need someone from robbery to take care of this stolen merchandise."

I explained to Maggie why her tenant was wanted as I opened the boxes in the living room. I pulled out a bronze statuette and a silver chaffing dish. Some small crystal animals were packed in newspapers. I had seen them on the Gardiner's insurance list.

"He's a thief, too." I held up a gold necklace strung with amber and jade beads. "Now, if I could find his gun, my job will be done."

Thundering footsteps rattled the stairs. I opened the door for the officers. "I have a gift for you." I indicated Baca on the floor.

"Is that the felon we were told to pick up?" the one named Jansen asked.

"This is Juan Baca." I helped Maggie off the chair. "He might have a headache."

"The bitch kicked me on the head," Juan snarled.

"Yes, I hit him but he locked me in a storage room and left me to die. I consider that tap on the head small payback." I drew back my foot to kick him again.

"No, no, no, lady." Jensen's partner stepped between me and Baca. "You can't kick him while he is cuffed."

"Too bad," I said.

"Before you take him, you need to check him for weapons. He shot a woman and we are looking for that gun."

"Is that his?" Jenson asked as he pointed toward the Smith and Wesson in my hand.

"No, this is mine. We had a moment before I cuffed him."

The officers stood Baca up and frisked him. They found a small caliber revolver in a pancake holster in his jacket pocket.

"Don't lose that gun," I said as they walked him out the door. "It might be the murder weapon."

I found Maggie in the kitchen cleaning out the refrigerator. "I don't think he'll be back, will he?" She wiped down the shelves and propped the door open. "What do I do with all these boxes?"

"Nothing," I said, opening another. "Someone from the Robbery Division will be here soon. Most of this stuff was stolen and there's a legal firm involved with returning it to the owners."

"How long do you think it'll take to clear out this stuff?"

"I'll let you know after I talk to them." I held the door for her.

Maggie started down the stairs and turned back before I could close the door. "Well, can I reserve the apartment for you?"

Chapter 21

"These definitely are part of the Gardiner furnishings," Albert Lorry said. He was the same law clerk I had met the last time we were in the police property room. It seemed like a month ago and he still wore the same green plaid slacks and yellow bow tie. "We'll see to getting this lot back to the mansion as soon as it's released by the police and the court."

"Have you recouped all of the furniture now?" I stared at the mismatched pieces. The scarred tables and chairs would need to be restored. Baca and his cohorts hadn't shown a lot of respect for the Gardiner's furniture.

Albert shook his head as he thumbed through the pages on his clipboard.

"We're still missing some of the smaller antiques and most of the glass pieces. We haven't found any of the jewelry that was taken from the company safe."

"Who had access to it?"

"That's a problem." He looked up from the clipboard and took off his glasses. "Several of the senior officers had the combination, but once Ronald Gardiner's death was announced, his office and the safe were sealed by the police."

"Sealed by the police means they put tape on the door." Even I knew how to get around that. "Did they check the contents before they sealed it?"

"No. They had to wait for a warrant." He worked the clipboard back into his fan-bottomed briefcase.

I wondered if he lived out of that case. Surely, he didn't have enough papers to cause that much of a bulge. I watched him pick it up and almost laughed when he tipped slightly to the side.

"What did they find in the safe?"

"It had been cleaned out. Apparently, Samuel Gardiner emptied it before he disappeared." He moved to the door. "Mr. Duke will be in contact." Lorry walked out listing to the left.

It was up to Jesse Duke's law firm to identify and return the Gardiner furnishings to the mansion. Some of the items had been sold and scattered from San Francisco to Los Angeles. The oddest thing the police found was a list in Margo's purse naming each item sold, the buyer, and the selling price. The police worked with the lawyers to locate the buyers to seize the furniture and return it to the current owners of the Gardiner Mansion.

Before I left, I met one of the detectives I saw on my last trip to the stolen property room. "I heard that some more of the Gardiner furnishings had been located from Margo's list. Do they have any recourse to get their money back?"

After the detective stopped laughing, he said, "No. If you think buying a Tiffany lamp for twenty dollars is a legitimate deal, you deserve to lose your money."

"Will all of the furniture be recovered?"

"Doubtful," he said. "They were cash sales and a lot of the buyers denied knowing what we were talking about."

I was grateful to be out of that end of the case. I had never dealt with stolen property while on the force. My beat was crimes against persons and, after going through this mess, I was glad I spent my time with the stabbed, shot, and bludgeoned.

"If the buyers ever put the items up for sale, we should be able to get them," he added. "Lists have been sent to antique dealers, auction houses, and pawn shops."

"What about the paintings? Have any of those turned up?"

"The art work may be easier to trace. Those dealers are very particular about what they buy and sell. Stolen art is hard to unload. The lawyers are handling that with our blessings. Do you have any more questions?"

He pulled on his jacket and held the door for me. I was being dismissed. I've been asked to leave before, but usually not so nicely.

****

The coroner released the report on the death of Ronald Gardiner. The swelling in his throat and airways along with some bleeding in his lungs indicated that he died of anaphylactic shock. His history of allergies along with the traces of bee venom found on his face and in his mouth were identified as the cause of death. Murder by person or persons unknown was the manner of death.

That explained the spraying sound Caroline heard just before her husband fell over. The abbreviated report I saw at the police station had listed heart attack as his cause of death.

Caroline's death was more obvious. A bullet through the heart spoke for itself. The cartridge had been traced to the gun taken from Juan Baca.

The Rand family invited me to the memorial service to be held as soon as the coroner released Ronald and Caroline Gardiner's bodies for burial. I had done my best to avoid funerals since my husband died. But my life had revolved around the lives of the deceased for what seemed like a dozen years, although it had been less than a month, I felt obligated to attend their funerals.

The paint Mandy sloshed on my clothes left me with nothing to wear to a funeral. I found a midnight blue shirtwaist at my favorite dress shop that matched my only pair of paint-free shoes. For years Liam's mother tried to teach me that a lady should wear a hat and gloves to weddings, funerals, and any other polite gathering. I can't stand to wear a hat and I don't own a pair of gloves. The best I could manage was to brush my teeth and hope for a strong wind that I could blame for my fly-away hair.

Jesse Duke, his law clerk, and the Gardiner Electric executives joined the family at the funeral chapel. It was obvious that the generic celebrant knew nothing other than the names of the deceased. One of the senior vice presidents gave a long-winded eulogy for Ronald, mentioning every minute detail of his business life. If he had done half of that, he must have had no personal life before Caroline came along.

Mike, her oldest brother, eulogized Caroline's life before she moved to San Francisco. Some of her friends shared their memories of the Caroline they grew up with. No one mentioned the broken engagement that had motivated her disappearance.

A couple of hymns and the funeral concluded with

the announcement that the bodies would be interred in the Gardiner family plot. There were no arrangements for a reception after the burial.

I had seen only the house and the immediate grounds. The private family cemetery was on the back side of the property behind a stand of Mediterranean cypress trees. It was a well-maintained peaceful stretch of land, hidden from the neighboring properties.

The small motorcade stopped next to a break in the trees. The company vice presidents served as Ronald's pall bearers. Dressed in black suits, white shirts, and gray ties, they looked like a flock of emperor penguins as they carried Ronald's coffin to its burial site. Friends from her high school bore Caroline's casket to the open grave. Each of the mourners was given a pair of roses as they followed the coffins. Scattered among the tombstones that memorialized various family members, we listened to a short Bible reading and a prayer. Everybody placed a rose on each coffin and the Gardiners were consigned to their final rest.

Chapter 22

Juan Baca accepted the deal. In exchange for a guilty plea for Caroline Gardiner's murder, the theft charges were dropped. He would be a guest of the state of California for at least thirty years with no chance of parole. After that, New Mexico wanted him for Ronald's murder. He was the last of the conspirators to appear in court. The others, his Aunt Margo, Samuel Gardiner, and their assorted helpers, were already sentenced and locked up.

Samuel had hired Baca to eliminate his brother so he could take over Gardiner Electric. Ronald's process for using nuclear waste to produce electricity could be used in areas where no other method would work had received a lot of attention. Ronald had decided to make the technology available to groups working in Third World countries at no charge. Samuel disagreed.

My job was done. I had found Caroline's killer and seen him off to jail, solved the robbery of the mansion, and found Ronald Gardiner's murderer. I had become so involved in the case, that now it was finished, I felt like I had nothing left to do.

I drove to Liam's condo. Max was still hanging out there. He had given up his apartment and put his belongings in storage. He found a vacant condo in Liam's building. He liked the extra space and, since he was on disability, he had time and a bunch of friends to help make it livable. Now all he needed was a cat.

I shook his foot. "You busy?" Max was sound asleep, stretched out in the recliner with Hobo curled up on his stomach. The stab wounds must be healed or he wouldn't be able tolerate the cat's weight.

"It's our nap time," he said, his eyes closed.

I picked up Hobo and dropped a hoodie in his place. "You need some fresh air."

"What makes you think that?" putting his arm over his eyes.

"Liam told me that your doctor wants you to get out more." I dropped his shoes beside the chair.

"Okay. Just give me a few minutes." He struggled to push the foot rest down. "Hobo needs his box cleaned." He reached down and pulled on his shoes.

"Seems to me like one of you big manly men could do this job," I said as I looked at the nasty mess.

Hobo watched me clean it out and hopped in before the dust from the new litter settled. I poured cat crunchies into his bowl and gave him a scratch behind the ears. "There you are, Hobo. You're fixed for the day."

"What's taking you so long?" Max called from the open door.

I grabbed my purse and followed him to the car. He walked so slowly, I looked like a bride stutter-stepping down the aisle trying to avoid crashing into him.

****

The trip to the Gardiner mansion required getting on the freeway. I had driven with Max before and he never let up on giving me grief about my driving. This time he sat with his head tilted back, eyes closed, looking completely relaxed. When we turned into the driveway, he straightened and looked around.

"Where are we?"

"The former residence of Ronald and Caroline Gardner." I pulled up in front of the house.

The building hadn't changed, but the grounds looked well used. Beaten-down grass marked a baseball diamond with actual bases rather than the couch cushions I'd seen in Needles. A broken window pane on the second floor was evidence of a foul ball. The toys strewn around the perfectly-trimmed bushes gave the house a lived-in look.

Mrs. Rand opened the door and invited us in. "You'll have to ignore the mess." She led us toward the kitchen. "Come on back. I'm working on dinner."

We followed the aroma of frying chicken and I peered into the living room as we passed. Tables, chairs, beds, and other pieces of furniture were stacked in there. A variety of knick-knacks were wedged in among the other things.

"I saw you looking at my mess," said Mrs. Rand. "I had the movers put all of it in there since the room is the size of a ballroom. I hope I'll be able figure out which item goes in each of the rooms. I can't believe that there'll be more coming."

"Did you receive a copy of the insurance papers from Jesse Duke? They document the room-by-room furniture placement that you could use a guide." I watched her take the chicken out of the fryer and put it in the warming oven. A couple of loaves of home-made bread sat cooling on the side of the stove.

"I really haven't had time to look at it." She pushed a damp lock of hair off her forehead. "This has been overwhelming."

"Are you trying to handle all of this without help?"

"The first cook I hired lasted two days" She took out a pitcher of iced tea from the refrigerator. She passed around glasses then sat down with us at the table. "She claimed my children were going to cause her to have a heart attack. The second one walked in and out in less than five minutes."

"Wow!" I couldn't think of anything to say. "Maybe Jesse can recommend an agency that can help."

"That's where those two came from."

"What about a housekeeper?"

"Same story except the first one saw the children in the front yard and turned around and left without getting out of her car. The next one walked in the front door and out the back door without speaking."

"Call and tell him to try harder." After all, he was being paid to help them settle in. "You might tell him to offer them more money."

Her oldest son limped into the kitchen, running a towel over his head, smelling of chlorine. He wore a pair of board shorts and a t-shirt with Stanford across his chest.

"You remember our oldest Mike?" asked Emily.

"Yes." I shook his hand and inclined my head toward Max. "You have something in common with this guy. The same woman tried to kill both of you."

They compared notes until Mike noticed tears in his mother's eyes. He hugged her and patted her back and invited Max to join him on the patio.

I handed Mrs. Rand a tissue and waited until she swabbed her eyes and blew her nose.

"I can't stand to hear him talk about the stabbing,"

she said between sniffles. "We were told she's locked up again and he shouldn't be concerned about her coming back. But I still have my doubts."

"I think the hospital staff has learned just how dangerous that woman is." I stood and signaled for Max that I was ready to leave. "The last time I heard anything was that they were trying to limit their liability for the mayhem she caused. They'll be lucky if they aren't sued."

Leading us back toward the front door, Mrs. Rand said over her shoulder, "We're just glad to have Mike back in medical school."

We paused at the entrance to the living room. "What're the pieces of paper for?"

"I used sticky notes to mark the furniture that I wanted restored. Some of the wooden pieces were badly handled." She pointed to the ripped settee. "Do you know what happened to this?"

I had to laugh. At the time those men were tying me up, it hadn't been funny. "The men cut strips out of the settee so they could tie me up," I explained. Then I told her the entire tale. "If you like it, you can have it restored."

****

Max and I left the Rands with their messed-up mansion. He suggested that we should take a drive down Highway 1 to Santa Cruz. It sounded good to me. With no pending cases, I could enjoy a leisurely drive down the coast. At this time of the year, the ocean was calm with waves rippling onto the sand. The crops and forest on the land side were spectacular because of the recent rains. If we stayed on this road, we could have dinner at my favorite seafood restaurant in Pescadero.

"I'm surprised that you'll ride with me," I said as we passed Half Moon Bay. "I remember you said that my driving was like a near-death experience."

"The comparison is invalid." He leaned his seat back farther. "Now that I've had an actual near-death experience, your driving doesn't even come close."

I had rescued a cat from the alley behind our house when I was in high school. He allowed me to feed him as long as I didn't pick him up. One night he was attacked by a raccoon. After a week in the animal hospital, his personality had mellowed. Much like the cat, Max's disposition seemed to have improved. He hadn't made a sarcastic remark in days. I didn't expect Max to curl up in my lap like the cat, but he was definitely a nicer person. And somehow, he and Hobo were friends now.

"Would you like to listen to some music?"

"Not now," he said, not opening his eyes. "I'm enjoying the silence."

"You have Liam's place all to yourself. Are you saying it's not quiet?"

"He has the last landline in San Francisco and it rings all day long."

"Have you checked to see who's calling?" It was probably none of my business, but Snoopy was my middle name.

"Mostly advertisements and pollsters and some woman named Alissa."

"Alissa who?"

"I don't know. Liam took her out once and she's still interested. He's not."

"What's wrong with her other than the persistent phone calls?"

Max ignored my question. We had passed the housing developments and now the cutoffs to the beach were on the right and farm fields on the left. He sat up straighter and pointed toward one of the turnouts.

"Turn in there." He rubbed his leg. "I've got a cramp. I need to get out and stretch."

Max stepped out and dropped his hoodie on the seat. I watched him work through the slowest stretching routine I'd ever seen. When he reached over to touch his toes, he didn't straighten back up.

"Did you fall asleep?"

"You want to give me a hand?" His breath rasped in and out. Sweat beaded on his neck.

I gave him a hand up and held his arm until he was steady on his feet. "You okay now?"

"Give me a minute." His hand shook when he let go of my arm. He wobbled a little then climbed back into the car. He was still breathing hard when I took the wheel.

"Can we head back to Liam's now? I've had enough fresh air."

That was the last I heard from Max until I parked in front of the condo. Liam opened the front door and watched us shuffle up the walk. I held onto Max until we got through the door.

"Where have you been?" Liam asked.

"We went for a drive down Highway 1." I gave Hobo a shove off the chair. "Max needed fresh air."

He helped Max sit in the recliner "What did you do, make him run part way?"

"No. That's what you would've done."

Hobo jumped on Max's lap, punched around on his leg then lay down. Both of them were half asleep.

Just then the phone rang. Liam looked at the caller ID and grabbed the receiver. "Do not call me again." Liam seemed to be listening, but I had seen that expression before. If I had better manners, I would've left the room.

"I don't want to talk to you, date you or have anything to do with you. Don't call again." He slammed down the receiver hard enough to crack the plastic. He poured two fingers of bourbon and downed it in one gulp.

"Another cop groupie?" I'm not sure but I thought I heard Liam growl.

"I made the mistake of going out on a blind date with her."

"And?"

"She was a high school cheerleader with blonde hair and a massive inferiority complex," he said as he poured another drink. "Been there, done that."

I got up and reached for my purse. "I hope she doesn't have any knives." Liam opened the door for me and I patted his arm. "When Max moves out, who gets custody of the cat?"

My phone buzzed as I stepped onto the walk. "St. James Investigations."

"I need your help." The voice sounded like an older woman with a slight middle European accent.

"What can I do to assist you?"

"Well." She paused, breathing heavy and muttering words I couldn't understand. "My uncle left me the key to a safe deposit box, but he didn't say where it's located."

"Do you have any idea whether it's in a bank or a private business?"

"I don't have a clue, but Miss Sylva is going to try to find out where the box is tonight. I'd appreciate it if you'd go with me."

"I can't meet with you tonight." I didn't want to turn down another case out of hand since Caroline's investigation was wrapped up. This might be worth listening to. "It'd be better if you'd simply tell me what she has to say and we can go from there."

"Miss Sylva said it was important for everyone involved in the search to be at the meeting. The united life forces will enhance communication with Uncle Daniel."

"Sorry, I only deal with the living."

A word about the author...

Born in a farmhouse in Rogers County Oklahoma, Inez grew up in nearby Vinita. Her education journey began at the University of Denver and ended at Oklahoma State University. She taught language arts and reading for thirty-eight years at the elementary, secondary, and university levels. Since retiring, she paints, writes, watches birds, and lives with a clowder of cats.

Inez is a long-time resident of Oklahoma City with two children and two grandchildren. She is active in Oklahoma City Writers, Inc. and an Honorary Life Member of the Oklahoma Writers Federation, Inc.

Thank you for purchasing
this publication of The Wild Rose Press, Inc.

For questions or more information
contact us at
info@thewildrosepress.com.

The Wild Rose Press, Inc.
www.thewildrosepress.com